MONSTER
MOVIES

Coming soon to a theatre near yo

MONSTER MOVIES

by

Brian Kennedy

To Megan

Contents

PICTURE START

FADE IN:

EXT. UNITED STATES

Birth of a Nation

FILM START — EXT. Space — the stars in their infinite multitude. We drift in the vast emptiness of the cosmos for what seems like forever. Psychedelic nebulas of stardust cloud the frame. High-pitched theremin haunt the upper registers resonating with the spheres. We fly past the Andromeda galaxy and the Milky Way appears swirling in all its majesty. DISSOLVE into our solar system and begin a LONG TRACKING SHOT through the outer planets — lifeless worlds made of plaster of Paris and held up by strings. We approach Earth and the deep sonorous echo of THE TRUSTY NARRATOR comes in from OFFSCREEN.

V.O. In the third decade of the 21st century…

SERIES OF SHOTS. Commerce marching to the rhythm of stock footage. Traffic lights signaling green. Automobiles moving through asphalt arteries. Car exhaust pipes vibrating with purpose. Skyscrapers towering like titans.

Antennas beaming out waves that float off into the skies. Telephone lines crackling with lightning. Interstate highways. Drive thrus. Gas station signs burning neon. The lights of the suburbs at night. Silent streets. Empty houses. CUT TO INT. Capsule — cramped with blue-filtered light.

V.O. …Mankind has now reached perfection and can live in peace.

CUT TO EXT. The beach — the end of the road. The sun goes down in a blaze of glory as men in white coats comb the beach with Geiger counters. CLOSEUP on roentgens shattering dials. The air becomes electric and the sea boils as THE MAN IN THE RUBBER SUIT emerges steaming from the ocean floor. A terrifying roar rips out on the soundtrack like an enormous door slamming in the depths of hell. The frames wind down to a crawl as he wades through the rippling waves of destruction. He's impersonating a monster, a giant evolutionary throwback but he's really a man-made disaster. Black columns of smoke ascend into the sky with SLOW MOTION flames groping after them. Klaxons and news bulletins scream while he destroys the city like a scale model — CLOSEUP ON the green glowing death ray and a scaly claw crushing homes in a gigantic rearrangement of all things — a swift and sudden change of scenery.

V.O. Quick, mobilize the Army. We'll show 'em what America can do!

CUT TO STOCK FOOTAGE from the last war. Firecrackers explode from toy tanks and airplanes. The monster screams out in pain. The man in the rubber suit FADES OUT and begins to turn up on late-night television broadcasts in-between commercials and severe weather warnings.

V.O. Will it ever be the same again?

FLASHBACK — PROLOGUE — EXT. Nothingness. The old gods arrive in their ships from across the gulf of space — faces obscured in LOW ANGLES. They disembark in an orderly fashion and assemble to survey the emptiness — CLOSEUP on hands twitching with the Protestant work ethic — CUT TO men shaping form from void — raising the facades of western towns — lighting the waving grass of windswept prairies for MASTER SHOTS — paving roads and carving sidewalks to delineate the world. CUT TO SERIES OF SHOTS — STOCK FOOTAGE from *One Million B.C.* — Devonian swamps on soundstages — paper mache volcanoes overflowing with gloopy mud — Iguanas with glued on fins and Armadillos with horns. LONG TRACKING SHOT across Monument Valley in the time of beasts — CUT TO the creation of man — a casting call — INT. Motel Room. A double bed with its sheets in disarray and Gideon's bible nowhere to be found. The only light comes from the static of the television and the neon burning through the curtains. THE PRODUCER sits on the edge of the bed talking into the camera.

Have you ever done anything like this before?

No...I…

Haaay, don't be scared. Why don't you come

over here, sit down? Relax a little...Did I tell you how *perfect* you are for this part?

CUT TO CLOSEUP of static droning — RCA Victor picking up the future and DISSOLVING INTO EXT. The shores of Plymouth Rock — a cold desolate planet. Day for night flickering into a grey dawn revealing tall ships laden with conquistadors, religious zealots, and blonde ingenues found at bus stops and drugstore counters.

V.O. And directly these invaders arrived, directly they drank and fed, our microscopic allies began to work their overthrow. Already when I watched them they were irrevocably doomed, dying and rotting even as they went to and fro. It was inevitable.

CLOSEUP on Petri dishes with slime molds blooming out hesitant veins DISSOLVING into dead pilgrims littering the new world.

V.O. These first humans, made of flesh and blood, were weak and unprofitable. It was time to go back to the drawing board.

INT. Laboratory. TRACKING SHOT across boiling flasks and colored test tubes. CLOSEUP on the face of THE YOUNG SCIENTIST, the rising star of Dow Chemical lost in careful calculation. FLASHBACK to the bathroom mirror with his double staring back and a deep silence between the stroke of a razor.

It's just a job. It doesn't make me a bad guy. *Right?*

END OF FLASHBACK — CUE orchestras swirling with industrial wonder and chalk dust raining equations as hands swirl chemical compounds and flasks boil over. Chemistry model kits form polymer chains that DISSOLVE into the second humans, molded from pulp paper, nitrocellulose, and polyethylene from melted green army men.

V.O. Necessity is the mother of invention and American Industry is the father of a new world.

FADE IN — dawn of man — EXT. West of the Rockies. Ghostly processions of wagon trains appear out of the rising sun, soundtracked to locusts singing their dense, blinding white frequencies in the tall grass. Cowboys in silver Mercury space suits ride out on point, cutting trails of melted green glass as herds of buffalo disintegrate in their wake. Movie ranches spring into existence and the frontier is flooded with industry types. CUT TO the heights above Bronson Canyon filling in for the Old West — A TWO SHOT of a pair of Indians cast as alien invaders foreshadows danger.

V.O. Here in the barren landscape of the West, a new mythology is written.

A heroic struggle ensues between THE SINGING COWBOY and the alien invaders — CLOSEUP on a silver revolver playing an insistent tune — sped up frames of stuntmen killing horses — bodies falling bloodless to the earth, again and again, the film devolving into an endless montage of violence — CUT TO CLOSEUP on blood staining white cotton and SLOWLY PULL OUT to reveal THE DYING COWBOY. He lays in the dirt, under cover of a boulder, using his good hand to steady his bullet grazed arm. Squeezing off a well-aimed shot, he grits his teeth and turns his attention to his leg — CLOSEUP on a broken arrow — he strips off his belt and sinches it around his leg as a tourniquet. A volley of shots ring out OFFSCREEN and a bullet ricochets with a cloud of dust near his head. The cowboy knows he can't stay here forever. Desperate, he stares into the sun for an answer that never comes. Hanging his head, he inserts his fingers into his mouth, letting out a sharp, soaring whistle that causes his pale horse TRINITY to MATERIALIZE by his side. Reaching up and grabbing the reins with his good arm, the horse drags him across the rocky ground into the safety of the caves of Bronson Canyon. The dying cowboy lays down to dream in the hollow dark — FLASHFORWARD — INT. A living room in the home of the future. The room is dark but for the light of a TV, a small twelve-inch projection set with rabbit ears. On screen amidst the static is the remains of the dead cowboy with his white hat, entombed, laying on the bones of his faithful horse, guns rusting and leather boots rotting — ZOOM IN on the empty eye sockets of the cowboy's skull and a fever dream blooms as a stomach-dropping tone drones out, soundtracking the slow spill of radiation that pools into the carpet. The words scroll across the screen — THIS IS NOT A TEST — and the living room grows impossibly white and silent — FADE OUT to twilight and the mushroom cloud rises over the rooftops. SERIES OF SHOTS — homeowners in the hills falling like perfect examples from education films, irradiated on their patio furniture, melting and merging with the plastic and vinyl — saucers on strings catching fire over Los Angeles — a Boeing serial number on a Minuteman — the square, uranium rotted jaws of dashing pulp heroes — noir shadowed men smoking malevolence and rapidly giving exposition — B-29's burning on the freeways.

V.O. Now it can be told! It is the story of a great and powerful nation, arising out of the pages of history. A grand play of overwhelming drama. A story with godlike cataclysms — giant grasshoppers — monsters in cheap suits — killer teenagers — alcoholic actors down on their luck earning a paycheck — burnt-out astronauts — and a cast of millions, faceless and anonymous. This vibrant world brought to you in vivid Technicolor — Aquascope — Terrorama — Spectorama — Astravision — Sexicolor — CinemaScope — Regal Scope — Cinerama — VistaVision — SuperScope — Techniscope — Naturama — Panamorph — Panavision — Scanoscope — Space-Vision — Spectrascope — Vistarama — Horrorscope and the brand new state of the art CineMagic technique. Filled with TERROR! CHILLS! and THRILLS the likes of which have never been seen on the screen before! All characters and events in this film, even those based on real or living persons, are fictitious.

CUT TO the man in the rubber suit walking with his hands splayed out in tension before him. A theremin shoots out from above — the bullets bounce off him — he stalks towards the screen — she screams — windows break.

     V.O. Attention personnel, do not leave your offices. Stay in place and hide under your desks. There is a monster loose.

     Flags fly at half mast and the national anthem plays at the sign off to static.

     V.O. Can you prove that it didn't happen? God help us in the future.

CUT TO: future -- past

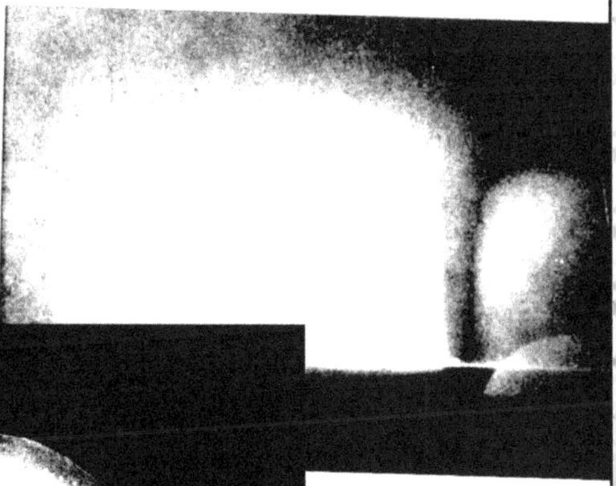

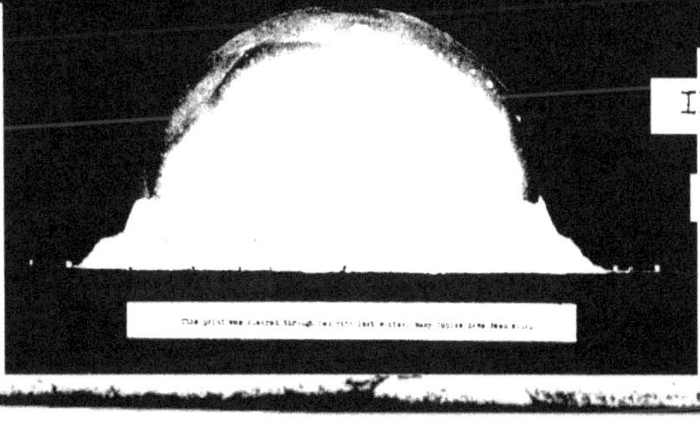

INTERCUT WITH:

radiation

&

Monsters

OPERATION CROSSROADS

The Movie Business

Now close your eyes and just imagine it — TITLE CARD — LIVE! FROM BIKINI ATOLL!

V.O.   It's Operation Crossroads! These historic experiments are a co-production with the US Army Ground forces, Army Air Forces, and the Navy in co-operation with the Manhattan Engineering District and many other branches of the United States Government and civilian scientific institutions. A spectacle like you have never seen — 95 target ships — 150 support vessels — a cast of over 42,000 — 104 still cameras and 208 motion picture cameras shooting 50,000 still pictures and 1,500,000 feet of film — equal to 11 Hollywood productions in the first few seconds of the blast.

Can you see it? It will be epic. One for the ages and gentlemen, I'm going to tell you right now and I say this with all humility and not an ounce of overinflated ego but you picked the right man for the job. I'm honored. *I really am.* I'm not blowing — forgive my French — blowing smoke up your asses, I am truly privileged to be a part of this production. This is as important to me as it is to you. The message — the real message of this picture — and it is one hell of a message — is so unbelievably vital in these times and you need the perfect picture to communicate it to the world. This has the potential to be huge and for it to be huge, you need a picture and you need it fast. More importantly, as we all know being old salts in this trade, you need a picture that *sells*. Something that gets 'em *in* — *asses* in the seats — eyes wide and glued to the screen — minds melted into the candy on the floor, eating it up and running back for more. Gentlemen, I can deliver that to you. I'm no visionary. I'm no artist. *Hell*, I ain't even a technical wizard but I sure know a thing or two about making a spectacle on a budget and that's why you called me because I've done this kind of thing before, maybe not as big or as expensive but I've concocted my fair share — BEGIN FLASHBACK — NIGHT — INT. Office of Statistical Control. The midnight oil is burning bright for MCNAMARA and LEMAY, the whiz kid and the general, as they sit across a desk from one another reading over tables and figures. A MONTAGE of combat mission ditch rates — effectiveness of nighttime low-level aerial bombing — wind pattern simulations of fires in wooden cities — medical case studies of the effects of jellied gasoline on human skin.

I want to wrap them up in fire Bob. Coat them in it, until the yellow bastards crisp.

The smooth hardened shell of brill cream can't keep the hairs on the back of Mcnamara's neck from standing on end.

Well, General, the numbers look promising. If the reality can match the estimates, we'll be looking at a true and decisive success.

Hell on earth, Bob?

Hell on earth, sir.

Statistical analysis. *Huh*. Hell of a thing, Bob.

Yes sir, it is, General.

My god. Imagine it. What will the future look like?

Lemay returns the cigar to his mouth and wistfully leans back to dream visions of a radioactive stone age — the East as a glass fused parking lot — quiet and safe but for the wind. Mcnamara straightens his starched Protestant collar and gets lost in his own reveries of the future. He dreams of data, rivers of it, flowing in from all fronts to feed an IBM Q7 that sprouts legs and plans to firebomb with efficiency. It aims to decimate with a will that the command and politicians lack — while the generals lay stoned on opium in their pleasure dome in the depths of Cheyenne Mountain — while chickenshit appeasement junkies plot for dominoes to fall — the Q7 sends telefaxes to every command base in the country — BRING THE WAR TO THE ENEMY. 49,000 vacuum tubes with no emotion calculate the cost-benefit analysis of jellied gasoline on children's skin. A 728 tape drive attached with an umbilical of magnetic tape scurries on its four stubby legs behind the Q7, feeding it maps and coordinates. Technicians scramble after all 250 tons of the sentient behemoth, picking up the spent tubes that pop off like hot kernels of corn. It smashes its way across the country, burning towns and holding no quarter until it reaches the West coast, where it wades into the water, disappearing on its mission to the far side of the Pacific. An AVERAGE JOE and JANE stand on the beach as the sun sinks into tomorrow.

Is it over?

It's over when we *win*.

END FLASHBACK and one hell of a picture. A moneymaker too — and while this may be a tad bigger, trust me, gentlemen, it's all the same. Now I have a few ideas. A couple of radical setups never before attempted. I want to do a long tracking shot with the dolly rig — OPEN on the edge of the beach with nothing but azure crystal waters in frame and start to move down the shore, slightly inland so we get sand — tide — palms come into view — exotica — a tropical Eden. And then BAM — center of the frame — ABLE in all his glory, glowing into a whiteout and we exceed the temperature of the sun. The radioactive cloud FADES INTO the dark spire of the Washington monument and the halls of the pentagon bustling with activity. Generals sit in the dark and review films of Hiroshima where the victims are lost in editing and an American actor looks bored in reaction shots. The lights come on to reveal a cheap office set with a flag and a rear projection view of the Capitol building.

Gentlemen, the primary purpose of the Bikini tests is to secure precise and accurate data so that we may further America's dominance in our new Atomic era — the camera comes in tight to a CLOSEUP of THE SECRETARY OF DEFENSE — the lessons we learn may save lives and many millions of dollars by guiding expenditures for national defense into the most productive and efficient channels. This is the objective of Operation Crossroads.

CUT TO a great ball on fire on the flat horizon of the sea that rushes toward the screen to form the title — OPERATION CROSSROADS — the brass fanfare FADES to EXT. Bikini Atoll from the air. Before the rain. An island paradise like no other — scenes from old westerns of peaceful Indian tribes living off the land — exotic animals lounging in the jungle — the fruit weighing down the trees. King Juda wakes at dawn from a dream.

They are coming. They will bring the future—

By the way, I got the perfect guy for Juda. Worked with me on a dozen pictures. Usually, I cast him as THE WISE OLD FATHER, the one who teaches the hero to shoot straight and respect the law, which is kind of how I see Juda. A noble father looking out for his children. My guy just radiates old nobility. We just bronze up his whole body and we're good to go. Anyway, we can talk casting later — CUT TO A WIDESHOT of the empty lagoon and the American fleet MATERIALIZES in a shimmering haze. VICE ADMIRAL BLANDY lands on the beach in a white linen suit and explorer's hat, transforming into STANLEY, shining the light of civilization on a dark spot of the world. He walks with purpose across the sand to the throng of natives who have never seen a white man and places his boot on the stump of a palm tree. The islanders regard him with awe — CLOSEUP of his Colt revolver holstered at the hip — Stanley pulls it like a quickdraw artist and fires it into the air.

Take me to your leader.

Jungle stock footage — explorers hacking through vines — deadly snakes hiss — wild cats yowl — OFFSCREEN the sound of drums begins and continues to get louder as we arrive at the village. A grand ceremony has been set up. Torches light the way towards a grand feast meant for the gods. Island women in grass skirts dance topless to choreographed rhumba numbers that reach a peak primitive frenzy. CUE Stanley and his men out of the bush — the drums stop — FREEZE FRAME on our intrepid hero — and then King Juda appears, in full ceremonial headdress like an Apache chief. His moves are regal and accompanied by heavenly choruses. CUT TO two hands entering an empty frame.

Dr. Livingstone, I presume.

King Juda and Stanley shake hands and introduce themselves because that's what men do and as they hold hands, Stanley smirks and flashes that Explorers Club rictus and Juda FADES OUT with his people into ethnographic films that will never be screened. CUT TO the brass shaking hands for the photo op. Now we have our setting, let's roll up our sleeves and be Americans — SERIES OF SHOTS — great big bulldozers plowing the earth — cranes constructing towers — concrete flowing — ships being loaded with supplies — sailors shaving sheep and strapping them down to the deck — target ships being anchored into place — crews loading down planes with cameras — the US of A singing. Through it all, we'll have the trusty narrator filling us all in like an insightful dad. We'll show the cameras being placed in position and explain how we're going to shoot this thing. Invite the audience into the making like we're all a bunch of real nice guys sharing something special with them — does great for the hearts and minds. CUT TO the science — INT. Laboratory — colored vials and Erlenmeyer flasks bubble and smoke dry ice. Introducing THE HERO SCIENTIST. Now, I know your lead scientist is some kraut fuck, *right*? Yeah, that's not going to work. Won't fly. No one will identify with a damn foreigner. Even one working for us. We gotta make a new character. Someone young and American, an aww shucks boy from Terre Haute or Wekaugen or some other corn-fed rathole — *No wait*! He's gotta be from out *West*! Arizona or New Mexico or the fame fields of Califor- nia. A man from self-made people who embody the frontier, an individual free from the tangle of East Coast roots. Yeah, I like that. He's smart and capable — he's a soldier *and* a scientist — he's a man who tempts the gods in a white lab coat — reckless and rugged as he lights a smoke with the bunsen burner — he slaps assistants for their lack of vision — he can crack the atom and be gentle in his love for his best girl. He's even willing to experiment on himself for the sake of the future — CLOSEUP of the hypodermic needle in his arm. It contains a green glowing plasma.

Ethics be damned! We must make *progress*!

He pushes the plunger and collapses to the floor. At first, his skin begins to project an aura of green light — wavelengths with sharp teeth that melt glass instruments and singe linoleum. He begins to fade in and out of the picture until he dissolves into a series of discordant horn blasts that begin a spree of terror throughout the area. CUT TO screams in the night and a CLOSEUP of claws dripping with blood — now don't worry, the victims won't be anyone important — no one you know — CUT back to the laboratory and we find him back as A DAPPER YOUNG SCIENTIST. Tell us, doctor, what does Project Crossroads mean for science?

In this 20th century world of atomic power, man is fully aware that he cannot assume an attitude of indifference to the new elemental force that he has discovered. He must study and understand the force that he has unleashed if he is to be prepared for the future and to that

end, Crossroads is a necessary continuation
of the experiments conducted at Los Alamos,
Hiroshima, and Nagasaki. All of our knowledge
on blast effects and radiological damage to
property and people come from these initial
forays into the forces of the atom. Crossroads
is an attempt to create new data sets that will
deepen our knowledge—

By the way, I know I'm getting ahead of myself
but I got to let you all know that I have some
great ideas for some sequels. Picture this —
CUT TO the previous scene — we just reuse it
and dub in all the relevant facts. We need more
concrete research into the effects of radiation
yadda-yadda-yadda, so in order to create more
data, we go ahead and bomb one of those shithole
jungle countries. I mean you guys are gonna
keep dropping these things and they're gonna
keep getting bigger, so I want you guys to think
WIDESCREEN — CUT TO a 20 kiloton airburst over
a rainforest packed with millions of subjects
just waiting to be analyzed. After the initial
blast, we wait about a week for the fallout to
spread and dissipate into a majestic glittering
fog that flows and caresses the surviving flora
and fauna. At night you can see it all glow like
a forbidden mystic city. Then we have our team
drop down from Sikorskies in colonial jungle
whites and pith helmets. The Joint Task Force
and A FRESH SCIENTIST make their way across a
blasted landscape, a caravan across a new lunar
surface — a Sea of Storms now calm and frozen.
No sign of life. We zero in on A NAMELESS
SOLDIER, a skinny, unsure fellow. He trips on a

scorched rock, falling to the ground, and acci-
dentally discharges his rifle into the back of
another GI — CLOSEUP on a sucking chest wound
— a buzzing hum as loud as high tension wires
rises all around them and out of a smoking
crater emerges a giant hissing insect inflamed
by the smell of blood. CLOSEUP on THE BEAUTIFUL
SCIENTIST screaming in terror.

*My god! The bulging cancerous eyes of those
insects!*

Irradiated and angry, the swarm kills off
everything in their path. They rampage in and out
of the blast zones, wrecking ruins and untouched
villages. Herds of people and animals stampede
through nature film stock footage, screaming
in terror as multiple green glowing legs crush
everything in blind hatred — FLASHFORWARD to
the end where the monster is defeated with an
ingenious new weapon in the soccer stadium, a
set that once cleared you guys can use for the
setting of the next junta you stage. Anyway,
that's the general idea. We don't have to think
the whole thing through now but rest assured
gentlemen, we can use that outline for multiple
pictures. Where was I now? Oh, so we go through
the science jargon — we don't really have to
sweat that stuff. Just throw it out there, get
it over with and move on. No details. Nobody
gives a shit about that stuff. I tell you, the
audience likes to *think* they're in on things
not actually *be in* on things — they don't want
to know the nuts and bolts or how the sausage is
made, they just want to know that they're not on
the outside, not powerless and with no control.

They want to think that they understand how things work, that they're not in the dark. You give them a little bit of light, just a tiny bit to see the paintings on the cave wall and they don't give two flying fucks about how they're made or how they got there — they're just glad to be inside and entertained *and* we are going to entertain them, gentlemen. One minute to H-Hour. EXTREME CLOSEUP on dead eyes — ZOOM OUT slow to reveal Vice Admiral Blandy.

The bomb will not start a chain reaction in the water, converting it all to gas and letting all the ships on all the oceans drop down to the bottom. It will not blow out the bottom of the sea and let all the water run down the hole. It will not destroy gravity. It will neither vaporize all the oxygen on Earth nor set it aflame. The bomb will not tear a hole in the fabric of time, petrifying us all in a single moment and leaving us frozen in fear for eternity. I am not an atomic playboy, as one of my critics labeled me, exploding these bombs to satisfy my personal whim. I am only following the script.

A funereal drone of high tension wires soundtracks the final SERIES OF SHOTS — members of the Manhattan Engineer District dressed in ceremonial robes anointing Able in parodies of ancient weird religious rites — CLOSEUP on THE FAT MAN'S curves — incense rises in the hangar — secret pornographic promotional stills of Rita Hayworth are projected upon the bomb casing and Able TRANSFORMS into GILDA — DEATH, the destroyer of worlds — palm trees in ideal weather conditions — Dave's Dream appears on the tarmac at Eniwetok — a ceremonial procession of black hooded scientists lead the bomb out of the hangar — the flight crew takes a knee — A SERIES OF CLOSEUPS on the faces of these brave pilots as they're illuminated by the soft plutonium glow — the bomb rises into the B-29 — a clapboard cracks TAKE 1 — the camera captures every angle of the B-29 in successive shots — ROLL SOUND as THE BOMBARDIER begins his log — CLOSEUP on a hand writing DEAR MOM AND DAD — CUT TO sentinels watching from the shore — cameras entombed in lead — empty villages and swaying palm trees like picture postcard exotica — CUT TO the ships in the target array resembling a ghost town — shaved pigs lashed to the deck CROSS DISSOLVING into theoretical victims of World War 3 — brand new Oldsmobiles, Mercury's and Plymouth's on the parking lot of the USS Saratoga waiting to be blown to Kingdom Come — the USS Nevada FADES OUT and reappears as a single story, two bedroom with the television in the living room acting as the designated aim point — CLOSEUP on the deep blue swells of the Pacific — 30 seconds to zero time — CUT TO the flagship USS Mt. McKinley 14 miles away — square-jawed sailors standing on deck, straight as arrows and gazing with unshielded eyes directly into the zero point. A whole MONTAGE of faces staring straight into the audience. Men of vision confronting them face to face. They are the men of tomorrow, ushering in an age of atomic warfare that they know will end in an age of atomic peace — and the audience is their awed witness. Gentlemen,

they won't know what hit 'em. The B-29 taxi's
out for the last time — zero hour approaches.

V.O. The motion picture you are about to see
is a fantasy of the near future.

The screen goes white and all that can be
seen are the scratches running down the film — a
clapboard snaps — TAKE 2 — a shot rings out and
the cowboy falls off the horse.

INSERT
CLOSE SHOT

scene 1

take 1

next
stop
EXT.
Hollywood

The Beginning or the End

CUT to the B-29 already in progress.

Dear Mom and Dad — Your little boy is going to be a star. I'm writing this 9,300 ft above the Pacific in medias res and I'm telling you to be prepared to see my picture in every paper and newsreel in the country. You're never going to believe it but we're going to drop the big one — an A-tomic bomb! This is one helluva big opportunity for me. Nothing'll be the same after this. Your little boy's big mission began late. Mission briefing at 0000. It was ok though, I couldn't sleep anyway — too much anticipation. I laid there all night in the pitch-black under a wall of humidity, going over all the drills in my head — DARK GLASSES ON — DIVE — 155 DEGREES RIGHT TURN — all the same moves, repeated over and over from Wendover to Tinian and I know them all. I am one sprocket moving within a crew that's been rehearsing for so long that I can truly say that we are a machine — a well-oiled mechanism waiting for the switch to be flipped — just kick us into gear and we'll take care of the rest. Yesterday, the whole crew was just itching for action. We dropped the L-6 like clockwork and taxied in on imaginary applause and ticker tape. We all knew without having to say it, that this was it — the last run-through — no more rehearsals — next time it would be for real. On the ground, THE CAPTAIN gathered everyone together and asked us to take a knee.

Men, we know what our mission is. We've been through it a million times but I want to remind you of the purpose of our mission. *You see—*

The captain then went to stand up and his sunglasses fell right off his head and cracked on the tarmac. But he didn't do anything. He just stood there and stared down at them — CLOSEUP on broken aviator sunglasses on the runway — and began to whisper to himself.

What's my line?

He kept repeating it over and over, under his breath like a mantra as he wandered off the airfield. He looked like a zombie from one of those movies — a sleepwalker under the hex of voodoo — half asleep and half awake, between worlds and cursed to navigate the narrow line of eternity. We lost sight of him as he disappeared into the shade of the palms. A patrol went out looking for him after he failed to report in but all those flashlights in the dark couldn't find hide nor hair. The crew went to bed not sure if the mission was a go but, *sure as hell*, the call came in at 23:30 and thirty minutes later we were all assembled in the briefing tent and lo and behold, there he was, spit-shined perfect like he was straight from wardrobe and makeup. A whole new man, ready to play his part. The briefing commenced at 0000 and our payload was revealed — an atom bomb — just like in the pulps. Can you imagine it, the future here and controlled by my hands — CUT TO me as FLASH GORDON himself, zooming in out of the stratosphere in that silver rocket, wiping those hordes of space devils off the planet with a blast of that atomic ray. A warrior out of the skies the titles scream — a knight in shining armor for the atomic age — hero of the new century. I guess if I'm Flash, I'll need a Dale by my side. I'll have to work on that when I get back. You'll both be happy to know that we ended the briefing with a special prayer from THE CHAPLIN.

ALMIGHTY FATHER, who wilt hear the prayer of them that love thee, we pray thee to be with those who brave the heights of thy heaven and who carry the battle to our enemies. Guard and protect them, we pray thee, as they fly their appointed rounds. May they, as well as we, know thy strength and power, and armed with thy might may they bring thy fire and fury to those that oppose us — burn them — vaporize them — exterminate them — wipe them from thy Earth, Almighty Father and show us the way forward — toward thy world yet to come. Allow us the use of thy great and awful swift sword, so that we may beat it into a plowshare that will till the field of a great tomorrow. In the name of Jesus Christ. Amen.

We got the engines going at 0227 and began to taxi out at 0235. On the outer reaches of the runway, we passed the burned-out tail sections and fuselage of other birds and I got the feeling that this was the last time — that everything after would be meaningless — that once the mission was complete, when the fires burned down to embers, when everything was in ruins, all time would stop — nothing would move forward — THE END. As we got off the ground at 0245, leaving black contrails in our wake, I said my goodbye to the world. Ain't that silly. Your little boy, as scared as the day he left home. I got to remember though — if I don't do this someone else will. I have to be strong. I have to try to remember what you always told me, dad.

Sometimes you have to do the unspeakable, son. It's just what men do.

I'll keep that in my mind dad, right at the center, on track to the target. These things have to be done. The Captain knows this, that's why he's sitting at my back, above me bathed in red darkroom light, gripping the wheel and staring straight ahead. CLOSEUP on unblinking pools of black — his vision is clear, any doubts that clouded him are gone. He now sees beyond the cockpit and through the dark, shutting out everything beyond his periphery because nothing else but the target matters. As I write this at 0300, THE WEAPONEER taps him on the shoulder to indicate his retreat into the bomb bay to begin arming procedures — and the captain doesn't move a muscle — not a twitch — not a word — not a blink — all he sees is a particle of dust laying at the dead center of Ground Zero. It's a long ways away but he's setting the course for all of us. I know that with him behind me, I can do what needs to be done. I can do you both proud. Back home it's still yesterday. I imagine you two are already awake and going about your day, unaware of tomorrow or what your little boy is doing. SERIES OF SHOTS — EXT. A white single-family home with a picket fence and perfect lawn — INT. Dining room, a table with red checkered oilcloth and dirty dishes — CLOSEUP on grease and drying egg yolk — INT. Empty garage — oil stain on concrete — EXT. Residential street — the driveways and sidewalks empty — EXT. Main Street — every shop window gleaming with a CLOSED sign — EXT. The movie theater — dark but for the marquee which reads — WE CAN DO IT. CUT TO EXT. The plains of Wichita — The Air Capital of the World — Peerless Princess of the Plains — The New Memphis of the American Nile. TRACKING SHOT across new Fords, Pontiacs, Chevrolets, and Oldsmobiles lining the road in a traffic jam that goes on for miles — the camera rises and a CRANE SHOT reveals their destination. EXT. Plant II — 2.8 million square feet of American ingenuity, a great temple of industry rising above the waving grass, the parking lot full of Superfortresses waiting to fly with workers streaming in from all directions — CLOSEUP on an assembly line of timecards punched with patriotic vigor — CUT TO the massive outer doors of the plant opening up towards the sky. INT. The bustling beehive. This is the battlefield of total war, a war of production the likes of which have never before been seen on the face of this Earth. An entire nation mobilized for one purpose — TITLE CARD — VICTORY — as industry sings on the soundtrack, the camera TRACKS IN and among the housewives assembling fuselage and the deferred husbands cutting templates and the retired inspecting rivets and the children changing cannon plugs, there you are in the middle of it all. Both of you, shoulder to shoulder, at the beginning of your second 10-hour shift, glazing the same cockpit windows that I stare out of now on my flight into the dawn. I won't let everything you've sweat and bled for go to waste. I'm not afraid to do my job. Your little boy is awake and ready to make you and the whole country proud. It's 0430 now and there's a late moon in the East. A waning crescent moon. A sign of an end and the promise of a new beginning — time ticks aways OFFSCREEN towards 0916 — and I am the instrument of that new beginning. Here I sit at the tip of the spear, a glass bubble with a pressurized aluminum war machine behind me, hurling forward toward the target. A 2600 rpm shiver drives its way through the vertebrae of my spine and I follow it as a tingling current along 10 miles of wire into A SERIES OF SHOTS of the bomb asleep, dreaming in multiple angles — your little boy asleep. CUT TO DREAM SEQUENCE — INT. My mother's womb — the black abyss of the ocean above me and the galaxies infinite and flowing beneath me.

She carries me with love and attention to the primary. My father ENTERS and follows stage directions — INSERT CHARGE, 4 SECTIONS, RED ENDS TO BREECH — INSERT BREECH PLUG AND TIGHTEN HOME — CONNECT FIRING LINE — INSTALL ARMOR PLATE — INSTALL REAR PLATE — and I am alive, eyes wide with visions of extras from Central Casting exploded and recombined at random — dying faces glimpsed in silent montages of devastation, their eardrums kicked thru and bleeding screams — uranium rind flesh — photo flash eyes that permanently see after-images only partially glimpsed in the residue of lightning strikes — shadows on concrete — roads paved in blood-soaked bandages — medical subjects cast for experimental films where I strike cities like obsolete sets — skyscrapers become singed skeletons — neighborhoods appear on lists of the missing — retail interiors remodel themselves into exteriors — schools transform into charnel houses — and the world adjusts to my imagi-nation as debris obscures the sky — glaciers melt and flood the coastal cities — forests burn — lakes run dry — and people cry through the streets, harmonizing with the whistle of roentgens through the worlds broken teeth. The end of this dream is already written. I have many others. In one dream I am a fat man, born from my mother BOCKSCAR, collapsing in on myself and leaving a graveyard with not a tombstone standing. In the blasted waste, the irradiated wind kicks up and a piece of paper swirls in a dust devil before laying down to die in the emptiness — CLOSEUP ON the letter — Dear Mom and Dad — as much as I deplore my actions, I cannot deny that I am a beautiful discovery and I can assure you that unless the world surrenders to me at once, my reign will increase manyfold in fury — CUT TO another life where they call me Gilda. I'm a huge spectacle — a movie star for the whole world to see — photographed like never before — captured in angles unseen anywhere else — the equal of 11 Hollywood productions in the first few seconds of my existence and all I do is play with toy ships in the bathtub while they take pictures. And I drift and spread on the wind — men in rubber suits haunt the frame — my sequels already written. I awake as DOG, inhaling desert sand and soldiers with my first breath and crying unpaid medical bills and bones with 10,000 year half-lives. There's one version of me where I arise out of the scorched earth as a giant tarantula, cheap and ragged, screeching jet exhaust howls as I lumber through ghost towns on my way towards civilization. Another where I'm diffused into a monstrous ant colony, quavering diseased theremin songs as I fight a war of extermination against the insects that run scared beneath me, pissing themselves in the streets. I am CHARLIE, born live as a broadcast, leaking out of vacuum tubes and pooling into nightmares that burn carpets in the living rooms of Los Angeles. I make my escape into the suburbs, irradiated and half alive, wandering half-built communities and un-finished roads. My uranium scarred hands find their way to the throats of teenagers parked on the highways — CUT TO two silhouettes in ash — shadows singed on concrete in foreign cities — educational films of silly turtles hiding under desks.

You'd better hide children. Next time it will be you.

The LOCAL POLICE CHIEF and THE ATOMIC SCIENTIST FREEZE FRAME in horror as it all comes back to them.

What have we done?

An all-points bulletin is issued.

V.O. Be on the lookout for an atomic monster — a crazed killer — an irrational beast — a figure of terror — description unknown — monitor all news for — kidnappings and missing persons — unsolved murders — alleged suicides — migrations of wildlife — thefts of rare metals and elements — strange phenomena such as flying saucers, strange odors that carry high pitched sounds, and unnatural things alive or dead.

I stalk the streets, lumbering from screen to screen with budgets of varying degrees. I travel in the land of the dead. My victims, both real and imaginary, remain unknowns — faces that flash horror, only to be lost in editing — gone and forgotten in the blink of an eye. I find them everywhere — in shadows and broad daylight — in city centers and suburban enclaves — in homes and high rises — in shopping centers, high schools, and military bases. Nowhere is safe. They all disappear in my hands — CUT TO NIGHT — the city vacant and silent — EXT. Back alley — crumpled leaflets lay scattered on the pavement — black cats run silent in the dark — a single bulb burns over the rear exit of a bar. I skulk in the shadows among the trash cans and broken bottles. The rear exit kicks open and a booze-soaked pile in the shape of a man flies out before it slams shut. Dirty rags pick themselves up and begin to stumble down the alley. Discordant strings rise on the soundtrack. My eyes become the camera and I MOVE IN toward my next victim — tensions rise as trajectories meet — I'm seen backlit as a malevolent black figure, claws raised to attack.

Hey...don't I know you?

CLOSEUP on a familiar face, grown distant and alien. I lower my hands and rack my brain to figure out that face. Where are you from? Where do I know you? And it hits me like a surge of electricity — the kid who manned the tail gun — what was his name? We stayed up drinking into the long hours on Tinian and shared stories of back home. He was from Omaha and had never seen the ocean until he'd flown over it. *What was his name*? I can't remember. I tell him, it's me, your little boy.

You don't look like him.

But I am him.

FLASHFORWARD to another life where I am no longer Death, Destroyer of Worlds. INT. Living room — dark but for the blue ambient glow of the television. A single recliner, an island in an ocean of beer cans, sits before rabbit ears wrapped in tin foil. I'm middle-aged, cirrhotic, and glassy-eyed, watching the late-night rerun

— the TV movie adaptation of my life. It stars AN OVER-THE-HILL "NAME" ACTOR as the captain and a couple of guys who used to be in westerns as the crew. I'm played by some FRESH-FACED ACTOR, a serious acting school type on the verge of breaking it big. He plays me as I see myself — an idealist — a patriot — a soldier — just following orders — no monsters here. There's a great scene where he says goodbye to his wife — some woman I've never known — right before takeoff. He grabs her and holds her tight.

Darling this mission is my duty even though it may rend the universe itself.

I don't care — TIGHT CLOSEUP on her tear-streaked face — everything can turn itself upside down and be swept aside but as long as you come back to me, *it will all be worth it.*

They kiss, the music swells and it never fails to bring a tear to my eye. The rest of the movie is bullshit — fabrications for drama — history with creative license. At 0816 the screen flashes white, the camera shakes and the actors ride out a shockwave on a cheap set — CUT TO grim faces and foreboding music — unspoken guilt floats freely through the air — CLOSEUP on the captain maintaining discipline.

That was the job boys. Now, let's go home.

CLOSEUP on the fresh-faced actor, unsure of his actions and his place in history — CUE patriotic hymns — CUT TO STOCK FOOTAGE of the B-29 climbing starboard into the clouds — and I get up to get another beer and imagine an alternate take — 0535 and we have low visibility on initial target and secondary. The captain and I flip a coin — the quarter tumbles in SLOW MOTION — heads, I win. Alternate target: our hometown. You and everyone we know will be destroyed — shadows on concrete — ruins in the stone age — unlimited glass parking. And I feel nothing. Time stands still and there is no future. There is only me — death with aluminum wings. 0730 Final assembly complete. 0850 we're locked into our bomb run. Won't be long now. 0915 over the target. We just need to make the turn down our street where it hooks West and then I can see our house. You are probably both out in the backyard, hanging clothes on the line and watering the grass. I'm sorry but the end is already written — THIS FRAME INTENTIONALLY LEFT BLANK — END DREAM SEQUENCE. I wake with the taste of lead in my mouth and I wonder about what I've done — it must be something awful big. Love to all, your little boy. P.S. You might want to keep this, it'll be worth something when I'm famous.

COMING ATTRACTIONS
ADVENTURE
SUSPENSE
ACTION

A MONSTER STALKS THE DESERT SANDS AS A MAN BECOMES A FIENDISH BEAST WHEN CAUGHT IN A NUCLEAR BLAST.

MANHATTAN DISTRICT

presents

MONSTER MOVIES

The Monster From Los Alamos

FLASHFORWARD to a new job and a new life. Different but the same. Sometime in the future. CLOSEUP of a scaly claw rising from behind the rocks — the monster already exists before the title appears — he's out there — alarm bells scream out over the soundtrack. EXT. Los Alamos Scientific Laboratory. A body on a stretcher is rushed to the hospital.

V.O. January 31, 1958, a television is switched on in Duluth and thousands of miles away, a South Seas island and all its people disappear under rising waves. Newspaper headlines across the country and the world announce the launch of Explorer 1 into space. And at Los Alamos Scientific Laboratory, a criticality experiment for the upcoming atomic test goes wrong. AN OBSCURE SCIENTIST, whose name is lost in the shroud of secrecy that cloaks our national security, discovered that day the dangers lurking in the heart of the atom. This is his story.

INT. Hospital. Colleagues of the irradiated scientist hold cigarette vigils and reflect on their guilt in the waiting room. THE LAB DIRECTOR holds hands with THE SCIENTIST'S WIFE while THE GENERAL keeps a reassuring grip on her shoulder.

If he doesn't make it, you can rest easy knowing that it was all for the greater—

A nurse bursts through the door gasping for breath and releases a foul toxic air of charred flesh, burning metal and circuits — a choking cloud that opens sores on skin — blisters like mustard gas — scarring lungs — the purple death from outer space floating through institutional green corridors. The lab director falls to his knees as his throat begins to swell and pulse like a diseased bullfrog. He claws at his deformed neck for air as the scientist's wife vomits on the choking general. The monster stumbles into the waiting room leaving a trail of burn dressings and death. The film wavers and he is lost in fever dreams of radioactive isotopes — cosmic rays fade in and out of him and he cries out in pain as he transforms back into THE DISFIGURED SCIENTIST.

V.O. I'm going to show you an educational film to explain what has happened to the poor man.

A SERIES OF SHOTS — Hiroshima victims — burial grounds for industrial waste — X-rays from the bodies of housewives with tumors of unimaginable size — photographs of abscesses filled with plastic — suburban housing tracts surrounded by landfills — deformed children from Love Canal — pools of glowing chemicals dissolving empty galaxies.

V.O. You see the patient has evolved into a new being, a future version of man. One who is suited to the tomorrow we are building — one that is unfortunately inescapable.

Do you mean, we will all be like *that* in the future?

V.O. I am afraid so. There seems to be nothing that we can do about it.

FLASHFORWARD. INT. The scientists study. Windows blacked out with tin foil. Books ripped in half and thrown from the shelves. Crumpled notes. A blackboard stands in the corner covered with failed equations. He sits at his desk, his face in bandages and his head in his hands.

What have I become?

CUT TO the highway at night. The disfigured scientist speeds through the darkness looking for a way out. He pulls off to get a drink at a roadside bar. The neon sign hums — THE BIKINI LOUNGE — the kind of place where you go not to be discovered. He opens the padded door and becomes bathed in a deep red light. The place is filled with regulars — defense contractors, film crews, and local business owners. A young woman stands on a piano in the back, bathed in spotlight, dancing silent and slow to a tinkling cocktail tune. The disfigured scientist sits at the bar and orders a Schlitz. THE BARTENDER pops a top and sets down a cold one. CLOSEUP on a sweating brown bottle that becomes the disfigured scientist mid-drink. The first swallow of beer, cold on a scarred throat, throws him down a hole with no air — a space disconnected in time where the movie just ended and for a long eternity, there is a moment to breathe.

You know somethin'...?

The film starts again as the average Joe on the barstool to his right, drinking boilermakers with that everyman — *I was in the service* — crew cut, turns away from the game on the TV, and stares at the disfigured scientist.

I want to unleash a wave of death and terror.

He speaks in the voice of a psychotic engineer, a steady rational tenor with hints of death camp designs and ballistic tests. He playfully slaps the scientist on the arm.

Someday. *Right*?

The man turns his dead stare back to the television where the game keeps going and nobody wins. The disfigured scientist goes back to his beer. He takes another pull off the bottle in an attempt to transport himself to nowhere when there's a tap on his shoulder. He turns to face A DIVORCEE IN A COCKTAIL DRESS. An unlit cigarette dangles from her lips. The disfigured scientist takes out his lighter and as she bends forward to meet it, he catches a glimpse of atrocities in the shine of her lips.

Blowing out a plume of red-tinted smoke, she begins to recite lines from a civil defense script.

You know honey, if a modern A-bomb exploded without warning in the air over your hometown tonight, your calculated chances of living through the raid would run something like this: should you happen to be one of the unlucky people right under the bomb, there is practically no hope of living through it. In fact, anywhere within one-half mile of the center of the explosion, your chances of escaping are about 1 out of 10. On the other hand — she leans in and lowers her voice seductively — *and this is the important point, from one-half to 1 mile away, you have a 50-50 chance.* From 1 to 1 1/2 miles out, the odds that you will be killed are only 15 in 100. And at points from 1 1/2 to 2 miles away, deaths drop all the way down to only 2 or 3 out of each 100. Beyond 2 miles, the explosion will cause practically no deaths at all — she fiddles with the scientist's tie and begins to talk in a playful pout — *naturally*, your chances of being injured are far greater than your chances of being killed. But even injury by radioactivity does not mean that you will be left a cripple, or doomed to die an early death. Your chances of making a complete recovery are much the same as for everyday accidents. These estima—

Her scene is interrupted by a shout from the other end of the bar.

Hey barkeep! I'ma have another old-fashioned!

A MAN IN A GRAY FLANNEL SUIT sits drinking with AN OLD MOVIE COWBOY still in costume. They toast the television and the breaking news that the Doomsday Clock is thirty seconds from midnight.

And I'll have uhhnnother beer — he tips his stetson up — Why not? Right pardner?

The man in the gray flannel suit toasts his newfound drinking buddy as their worst fantasies, long hoped for and unspoken, take definite form. Hiroshima explodes and its cloud of ghosts rises above an American city in footage repurposed yet again.

Eat, drink and be merry because tomorrow *they* are gonna die.

The disfigured scientist puts his head down and shuts his eyes. He wants no part in all this but complicity is a hard thing to dodge.

CLOSEUP on the face of the bartender.

Have you seen the future, brother?

The disfigured scientist falls off his barstool and scrambles to his feet. He backs slowly out of the bar and through the padded door. The morning sun hits him like a spotlight and he twists into a CLOSEUP with his hands over his face. Caught in the light of day, the atomic scientist is a demon — a ghoul — a beast — a monster — CUT TO CLOSEUP of the vampire's fangs dripping with blood — CUT TO the werewolf ripping flesh — the day inverted into a night shot — the bodies laid out in the filtered sunlight — shadows burnt on the sidewalk — from hell it came — the creature walks among us.

So, what was it doc?

Hmmm. The jugular veins, the carotid arteries, the esophagus, and the trachea were cut straight across. There was a complete transection of the spinal cord. In short, the heads were severed from the trunks. Death was instantaneous. Only a beast could have done something this horrendous.

A diseased shadow moves through the streets after midnight dissolving into daylight stock footage of Main Street commerce. Repeat of the earlier shot — CLOSEUP of a scaly claw rising from behind the rocks.

The tests are conclusive. The large fish scale we found at the scene of the crime is radioactive. There's no doubt about it. The sample we found at the crime scene is similar to the structure of Diplovertebron. A prehistoric amphibious reptile thought to be extinct. Fossilized specimens have been found near here in the ancient seabeds of Los Alamos.

The monster stalks the halls in darkness — heavy breathing fogs the soundtrack — the monster dissolves into car exhaust on endless concrete — blackened footprints appear in the valley and beyond — peculiar television images preceding disasters begin to appear with an attendant spike in radiation — a slow drip is heard as the polar ice caps begin to melt offscreen.

A WELL-TO-DO REPORTER presses record on a reel-to-reel and turns toward the camera to deliver his final monologue shadowed in flames.

This recording is for the future. My hope is that someday it will be found. All time has stopped here in Los Angeles. A monster of unimaginable horror has slouched its way out of the South Bay and is leveling the city. The blast of his atomic breath ignites the city like a scale model. I wish I could convey the terror we feel at this moment. The city's defenses cannot hold out for very long. Say a prayer for us — a prayer for the whole world.

CUT TO:

EXT. the future

CUT TO:

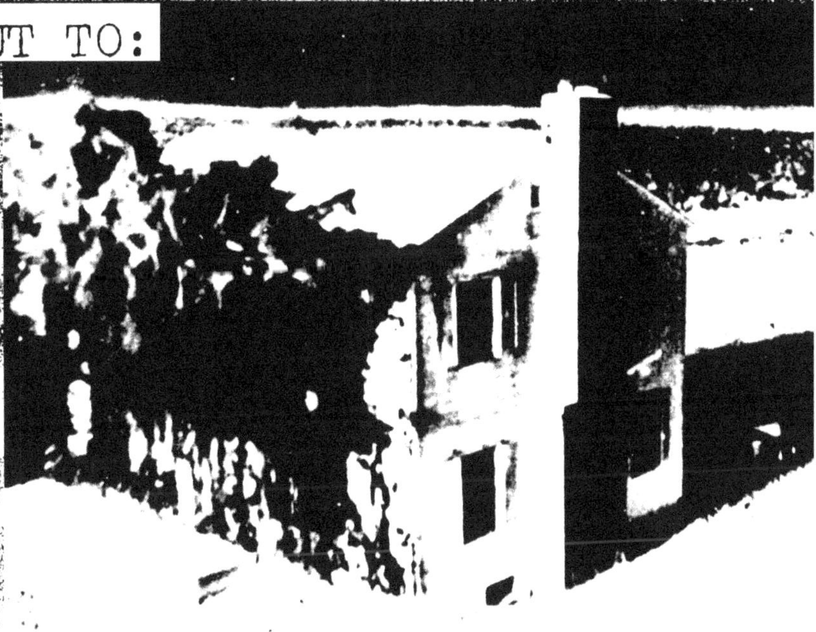

EXT. the future

DISSOLVE:

The World of Tomorrow

I know what I saw. I'm not crazy. I'm not like those people you read about, those weirdos who see little green men and saucers in the — LONG PAUSE — what I saw was real. *You have to believe me*. I know that's not easy. I mean, if I was in your shoes, I'd just assume that I was some sort of crank too. Another one of those raving loons on the street corner — someone to turn away from — someone to close the book on — someone to file away in a place to be forgotten. But I'm telling you *I saw* what *I saw*. Really. I know I saw it. I know it with every fiber of my being. What I witnessed was *real*. I can see it all — *right now* — all of it as if it were a film projecting inside my skull — all clear and in focus. The FILM STARTS right before it happened. I can see myself as THE BELEAGUERED FATHER, head heavy with the weight in a CLOSEUP that ZOOMS OUT, and there I am in the backyard, watering the grass and wondering what the hell the future holds. That was me. I was laid off that afternoon — LONG PAUSE — came out of nowhere. I worked at that plant for ten years. Ten *fucking* years. Loyal like a goddamn soldier. Can you believe that? *Ten years*. Shit, I was part of the crew that helped roll out the first Skyknight and after ten years they let me go like it was nothing. Foreman came up, told me to stop my machine and come with him — said THE MANAGER wanted to see me. Walked me to the office, opened the door without stepping inside, told me to sit down, and had the door closed before I even had a chance to realize there wasn't a chair in sight. I just stood there in that office while that sonofabitch manager sat behind that grey metal desk like the blob that he was — deflated and dripping mucus and shit from out of his short sleeves and stained collar. I tell you, in ten years of working out on the floor, I think I might have only seen the guy twice and even then it was from far away. Never put much thought into how he looked but right then and there, standing in that office, not more than five feet from him, it hurt to look at him. My eyes watered and I lost all focus. I ended up staring at the walls which were wood panels with all these MANAGER OF THE YEAR plaques and delicate paintings of hunting dogs. The whole time, he spoke this…*alien language* — this low-pitched waveform, so distorted that it was indecipherable — while the puddle he called a head pulsed with a blue reactor glow. He droned on for who knows how long — I lost track of time but when the glow and the noise ceased, I knew it was time to leave. I picked up an envelope from the desk and walked out of the office feeling as if I were about to fall into a black nothingness. I spent the rest of the afternoon just driving around town. I didn't know what else to do. It was like I was in some other world. It was all so new — and you know, now that I'm talking about it, saying it out loud and all — I realize that was when it started — when everything began to feel…so *unreal*. I remember cruising in SLOW MOTION past North American and Wyle Labs and there was this strange glimmer in my peripheral as I drifted by Aerospace Corp. I stopped at Hughes Space & Com where they're pumping out satellites in the bones of the old Rambler plant and it was there that the thought came to me — that *this was the future*. That's where I was — the future, it was right there and it was being built by my neighbors and my friends. Do you understand what I mean? They weren't building a world yet to come — a world out there like a mirage on the highway — they were building a real one. As real as you or me. A new world in the form of a gigantic ship, made up of production plants and test facilities — the winding roads and serpentine freeways were the circuits wiring it all together and the Standard Oil refinery with its miles of piping and distillation columns was the great rocket engine, flaring and blasting off into tomorrow. And there I was, outside the gate like a kid waiting for a spaceman's autograph. It all DISSOLVED together as I drove the streets. I came to my senses parked alongside the runway at the airport, listening to the planes take off and land. It was quitting time, so I headed home and acted as if everything was fine. Didn't have a clue as to how to tell my wife what happened, so I just played the part of THE TIRED HUSBAND. *Just another day at the factory, hon*! I sat silent through dinner while my wife and son played out the scene — INT. Typical American home, the sound of laughter can be heard as the camera tracks through the hall and turns into the living room, perfectly dressed with a new television and living room set from Sears — the camera continues over the couch and moves to the INT. Dining Room — a typical family meal at a small square table — glazed ham with pineapple slices, mashed potatoes, peas, and a lime Jello-O salad — DAD sits facing the camera, flanked by MOM and SON — CLOSEUP on laughing faces and smiles like out of the movies, projecting warmth and happiness in every frame. They were perfect. If I could, I would watch that scene over and over on an endless loop, because I knew then, that we weren't going to get too many more chances to play it. Final paychecks only stretch out so long. Unemployment doesn't last forever. Someday it would all end. I excused myself to go water the backyard and I went out and stood barefoot in the grass, spraying water at nowhere in particular. I loved that backyard. Facing away from the house, you had a WIDESCREEN view of the western sky, a great wide panoramic picture. You could stand out there and it felt like you could see forever. That evening, the picture was being cut right in half by a contrail in the sky. It was immediately after the sun was gone when you got that big expanse of deep blue right before the dark fades in and that contrail was

the most impossible white. An immaculate line,
drawn in the sky. And all I could think about
was, why can't that be me up there? Why does
everyone else get to move on to new worlds while
I get left behind? When would it be my turn? Why
was *this* my life? I stood before the open sky
and watched the contrail of the rocket and
wished I was leaving for a distant system too.
I felt that gnawing inside that hollows you
out, transforming you into a ghost to drift
forever on this dismal world. I looked up into
the sky as it grew dark and felt so lost. And
that's when it appeared on the horizon. At
first, it looked like a bright star that just
grew in intensity but I realized it was coming
closer — slow and luminous — and then there it
was, a saucer as wide and as tall as a mansion
floating on lights above me in the sky. I
remember wanting to call out to my wife, to have
somebody beside me, a witness to this vision
but just as the thought came into my head, the
lights from the saucer bloomed and enveloped me
in a spotlight of ice and stars — an impossible,
bright light that you could see through closed
eyelids — exposing every part of me and perme-
ating every cell. It was as if the headlights
of an oncoming car were about to hit me head-on
but right before the impact, it atomized and
left me naked and stripped of all thought in the
afterglow. In the SLOW FADE TO BLACK, the world
disappeared — birdsong ceased in the trees —
the planets stopped — the mountains eroded into
dust — the stars died and then there was nothing
but me — an inner space of timelessness with no
shape or form. I spent an eternity in the dark.

I was emptiness. Everything voided and unceasing. And after untold eons, I heard a thump — a quick, muffled thump that repeated itself a millennia later. I could sense that it came from below and I realized that I had dimension and a body. I became aware of speed and my movement through space. I was seated with one hand on a wheel and the other over my eyes. Without sight, I could feel myself running away down some alien highway, lit only by stars — there seemed to be no end and it was beautiful. I lowered my hand to the steering wheel and opened my eyes to the green glow of the dashboard. I was in my car driving along a starlit highway with a woman that seemed to be my wife. The lines of her face were slightly askew as if she were being projected at an odd angle back onto herself like a film inexpertly screened. When I looked at her I could see Super-8 home movies play across her face at 18 frames per second — her smile at the beach in CLOSEUP — her cheeks glowing in the light from the candles on my son's birthday cake — her eyes, washed out and overexposed in our backyard. She stared straight ahead and we didn't talk. I just drove on with the radio static droning. My headlights were off but I could see by the starlight that outside the car was a vast desert and off the highway, beyond the hills were the twinkling lights of far off cities — radiant cities of the future — towering utopias with buzzing skyways and symmetrical lines of glass and steel, veined by motorways for conveying citizens of rational geometry — great collective dreams just beyond the darkened hills — out of reach. Through the

car window of my mind's eye, I could see a
center — a giant metropolis of gleaming
crystalline perfection, where all roads lead to
a grand illuminated monument dedicated to
unknown architects — the visionaries that mapped
and built these cities of forever, their likeness
memorialized in stone and covered by a tarp
that flapped slowly in the wind — their faces,
their identities hidden from me. I was on another
path and the lights faded into the rearview.
The only thing visible was the road ahead. We
kept driving, for how long I don't know, the
ribbon of highway rolled on ahead in the endless
night. It was like a film strip, feeding itself
beneath the car and into me. I was the projector,
each moment a single frame one after another —
an illusion of continuous movement — always
forward, towards the end of the movie. As the
static began to rise OFFSCREEN, my wife pointed
toward an off-ramp and I exited onto a road that
began a slow descent. The stars began to wink
out one by one and the static became louder. The
road continued at a steady downward grade and
lead straight into the mouth of an enormous
cave that began to wind and cut back, spiraling
down to ancient depths with tunnels like the
endless hallways of ruined temples that ran for
millions of miles with openings all over the
world — their labyrinths leading to caverns
containing great citadels made of giant matte
paintings on sound stages with cardboard
boulders and stalactites, lit by red bulbs and
soundtracked by roentgens screaming. We passed
a billboard that said QUIET ON SET and I pulled
over at the next gas station, a Texaco burning

in the permanent midnight. I stood outside the car and could see it all laid out before me — EXT. Survival Town, USA — the new Atlantis — Lemuria sunk down beneath the planet — dark nowhere streets — empty shadow burnt sidewalks — neighborhoods of empty houses and overgrown lawns — living rooms with singed carpets and burning televisions draped with SLOW MOTION curls of smoke — the ship of the future, crashed landed and smoldering under the ceiling of the Earth. I turned and looked across the roof of the car to find my wife staring back at me in headscarf and sunglasses, our Grand Canyon trip playing on the screen of her face. She pointed forward and we got back into the car and followed the road into town. Off the main street, every route was blocked by heaps of scrapped B-29's and Studebaker's. We passed a ditch filled with casualty dummies, blackened and melted into the shape of their mass grave. We saw bombed-out shopping centers fallen into ruined temple complexes. To my left were single-family homes reduced to kindling and to my right were the glowing remains of factories. Every shop was a ghost town. Every home, a disaster area. Every street, a deserted runway. Not a soul to be seen. I began to wonder where the inhabitants of this terrible place were — who lived in this blasted landscape? As we drove on I saw in the rearview visions of a subterranean tribe — a race of mole people buried even further beneath those abysmal streets. Locked behind blast doors in AEC shelter caves, mutated beyond human recognition with gangly limbs and giant scaly paws, their tiny paranoid eyes blind with fear.

I watched them skitter about dank cave floors, clawing at each other among the skeletons of their dead — fighting to subsist on earthworms and untapped pools of crude oil. They were pathetic creatures cowering in the dark, listening to the sweet crying of sequin-dressed ingenues praying for apocalypse — inhabitants of a dank and miserable hell of limestone that reverberated with laments for the continuity of the sun. It all sent a chill of cold electricity down my spine. You want to imagine that the underworld is filled with demons. That it's a world populated by hellish creatures imbued with dark righteousness, meting out punishment to the wicked whose evil is obvious and recognizable. I wished with all my being that there was some gibbering monster with slime wet skin, salivating for blood in that massive cavern — some *thing*, violent and scary — biblical and full of meaning — anything but those silent streets and those pitiable things below. And you know, it was in those thoughts of hell that it occurred to me, that didn't people go down into the underworld to retrieve something — weren't heroes questing through Hades to find a lost love — to hear the voices of the dead — to get home? What was I doing here? What lesson did this vision teach? As if by answer, the main street ran out of pavement and turned into the green glass of a desert test site. Trinitite crunched under the wheels and the roentgens sang radio static. Ahead was the coral fence of a ranch. My wife pointed to the open gate.

They used to shoot westerns here.

EXT. Movie ranch. We pulled into the main dirt lot and parked amid trailers for the various productions. Stagehands, AEC bureaucrats, and the crew of Joint Task Force 132 lounged about, in and out of a circle of wagons waiting for the next set up while cowgirls practiced rope tricks and singing cowboys rode in off the wasteland to croon theremin odes to the stars. My wife took my hand and I could feel myself moving through sudden dislocations in space and time — EXT. Tranquility Base — Fort Apache — Futurama — Hiroshima — O.K. Corral — Southdale Center — Metaluna — Shangri-La — Venus — Dodge City — places familiar and foreign. Standing sets used and reused, facades shaken by dust devils, piled high with tumbleweeds and populated by vampires, diseased husbands, slimy Neptunians, Communist infiltrators, werewolves, bombing victims, unproductive Americans, and others unnamed and destined to be destroyed. We floated through ghost towns with dry mines and extinct malls being used for the end of the world — hollowed-out factories as the interiors of spaceships — cracked and overgrown parking lots used for wide-open prairies. We passed through a gothic wood in a deserted supermarket filled with fake trees and fog machines where the crew complained that they had only 20 grand, six days for shooting, and no guarantees on a next project. Things are the same all over, I thought as we were rushed into makeup and told not to speak to the talent. EXT. Vasquez Rocks outside of LA, the set of some sci-fi trash. Actors with diving equipment and fishbowls on their heads stood with a man in a rubber suit, sweating under the lights. My wife and I were extras playing a race of primitive aliens with no knowledge of the American way of life. We hadn't read the script and our motivation was unclear but the crew pushed us into place under the blinding lights as the director yelled action. The actors struck awkward poses under the weight of their costumes as the creature menaced ever nearer. When the creature reached THE STOWAWAY REPORTER, she let out a shriek that died into silence as the rest of the actors froze on their marks. OFFSCREEN the director yelled cut and everyone threw their hands up in frustration — the scene was blown, how I don't know but THE SECOND BILLED ACTOR blamed me and flew into a rage. He reeled across the set, drunk and looking to fight. The production assistants held him back until he gave up and stumbled back to his trailer. He took one last swig and threw his bottle high into the air in a parabolic arc that mimicked a rocket's trajectory before it shattered in a crash that killed three astronauts — stagehands entered from OFF CAMERA to extinguish the flames — flags were delivered to the widows in a scene deleted from the final cut. My wife and I were thrown off the set and recast in different films — she got the part of THE HOUSEWIFE OF TOMORROW in an industrial musical and I was cast as a grunt in a Defense film. As we were shuffled off to different locations, she waved goodbye — her face in CLOSEUP projected the despair of a home movie I didn't recognize. I recognize it now, but — LONG PAUSE — but now I guess it's too late. Can't change the ending. I was taken to wardrobe and outfitted with army fatigues, a helmet, pack, and rifle. I was playing my son, a soldier in a war yet to be. In the dark before dawn, men mustered in shadows. Fear covered their faces as we were loaded like cattle into trucks headed for ground zero. We started north from Base Camp Mercury and up through Checkpoint Pass where desert winds coming off the basin below brought the acrid smell of burning wires and television static — EXT. Frenchman's Flat.

V.O. Get in your foxholes. Get your goggles on and keep them on. Do not look directly into the flash until after the shockwave passes over you. Look *down* and stay *down*. It's going to be quite an experience boys.

30 seconds to H-hour. I could hear a slow drip as the polar ice caps melted OFFSCREEN. A SERIES OF SHOTS — old industry with brick chimneys waiting to be toppled — fully furnished, single-story ramblers and brick houses plucked straight out of the suburbs — Joshua trees with their hands fixed in the air giving praise to the sky — B-17s and F-10s at oblique angles, some facing head-on, some turned away, parked in the sand like a sculpture garden — the seas boiling — a forest of evergreens, uprooted and ready to burn — the Earth buckling and cracking open into immense fissures — motel walls built of brick, mortar and concrete — the shot tower silent like the skeleton of a colossal monster — the stars falling from the sky and soldiers shivering in foxholes waiting for the sun to rise. CLOSEUP on my face as it cracks with

anxiety. FILM LEADER COUNTDOWN — 3 — 2 — 1 — I poured sweat and began to shake to pieces — FILM START — I clawed at the dirt like a trapped animal until I found a hold and pulled myself out of the foxhole. I ran like a madman through a darkened studio, escaping only into new shots and different angles, each one capturing me again and again in flight. I pressed up against the screen and realized there's no way out. I faced the tower in the midst of the blast, hands thrown up for cover. 19 kilotons illuminated the dry lake bed and I became translucent, the blast wave distorting me into a wavering ghost. The desert floor and I were sucked up by the afterwinds into the stem of the growing maelstrom. Survival Town was blown up and away — paint disintegrating on celluloid in education films again and again — missing frames — censored scenes replaced with countdown reels and film leader — FILM START — NIGHT — I woke up under- neath a fallen bookshelf, buried under pulp novels that disappeared into floating embers. I crawled on my belly out of the debris, clawing through ash with lungs heavy and painful with the taste of lead. I stood up and took in the new world — all points of the compass a green glass parking lot that stretched on to the horizon. The remnants of houses smoldered. The tail section of a B-29 burned in the distance. Majestic clouds with sharp edges drifted in the black as the constellations burned in the sky. I looked down and my feet were wet, the hose drowning the grass in the backyard of a house I could no longer afford. I was right back where I started — back home in the future. I could hear

my son crying somewhere OFFSCREEN as my wife
came out and hit her mark beside me.

   Something's wrong.

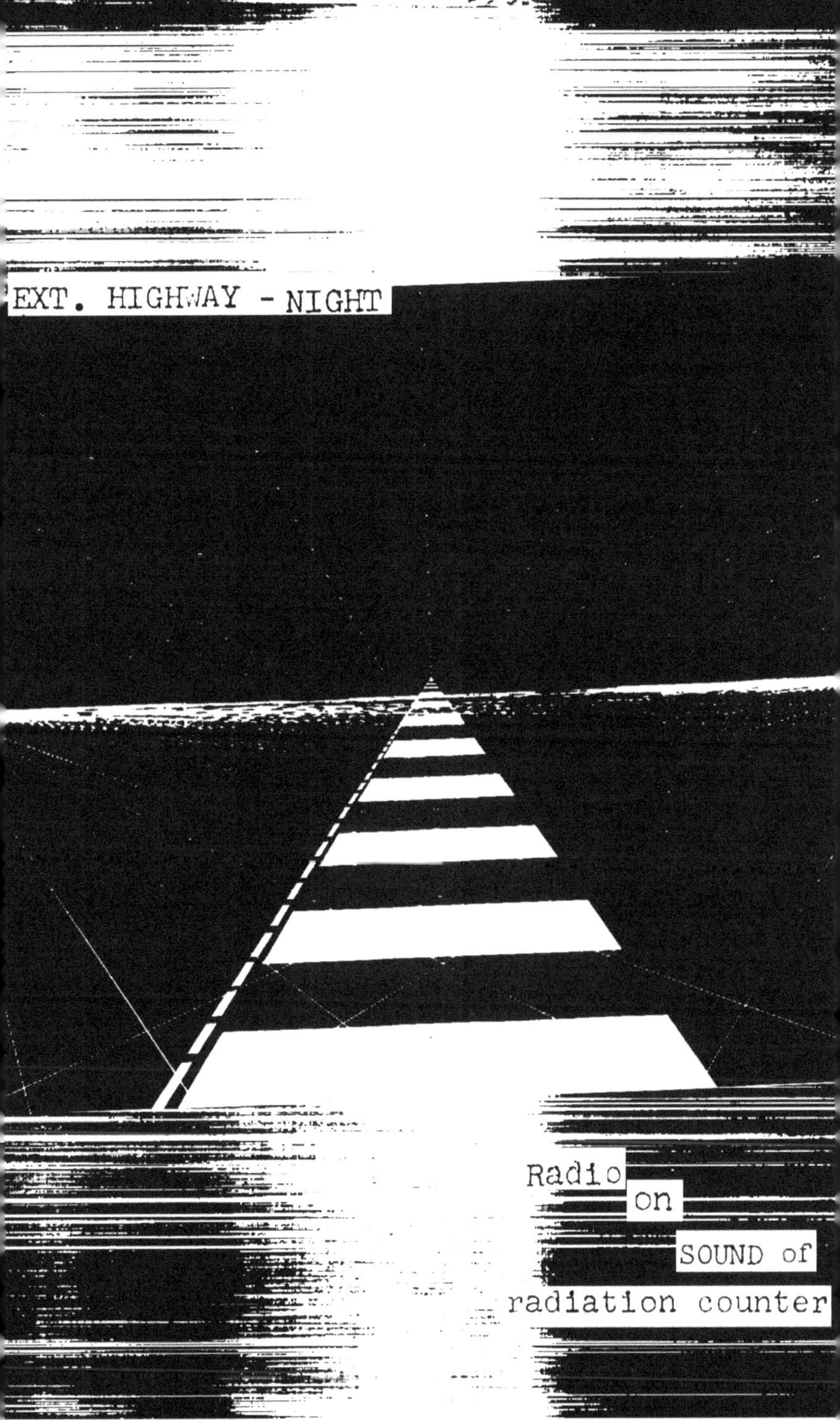
EXT. HIGHWAY - NIGHT
Radio
on
SOUND of
radiation counter

319   FULL SHOT

B-26 PRACTICING LOW LEVEL ATTACK on a Holiday Inn

Bay of Pigs TAKE 2

EXT. Space — stars in their infinite multitude — FADE TO BLACK and the smell of vomit.

Fuck — LONG PAUSE — let's start over.

INT. Bathtub — the drain is clogged and the tub is filled with an inch of dark orange urine and blood-streaked puke — CLOSEUP ON a patch of watery shit floating around a foot — stars FADE IN again and hang over the scene.

I hear the planes roaring overhead.

CLOSEUP ON piles of bottles on the bathroom floor — Old Grand-Dad — Old Overholt — Old Crow — Old Taylor — some broken, all empty.

I once played a pilot on tv.

CUT TO bathroom mirror autographed in blood.

Wait...no. I played a pilot in a *movie* that I saw on...tv.

CLOSEUP ON the sick bloated face of THE FORMER ACTOR, stars FADING OUT slowly.

Or did I just see a movie about a pilot on tv? Fuck, I don't know. Either way...there's this movie where this pilot — *who looks like me at least* — is in this experimental plane or — BURP — jet and he's streaking across the sky just like they're doing up there, right over this barren ass desert. It's like a test ground or something. So I'm…or he's blasting off into the stratosphere — wild blue yonder, *climbing high* into the sun, here I come zooming to *meet the thunder, at 'em now, given' it the gun* — and I crack that last sphere and it all goes dark. Dark beyond all sense. Nothing...absolute nothing — LONG PAUSE — but then there's this pinpoint of light, straight ahead like a light at the end of the tunnel. That's my destina-tion. And right as I lock onto it, this glow from behind me starts growing and—

OFFSCREEN — MUFFLED — housekeeping?

Noooooooooo! Shit...how many times...anyway. Where was I?

The former actor picks up the nearest bottle within reach and examines it for the slightest drip before dropping it back into the pile of empties. He reaches forward and turns on the shower. As he stands up to meet the cold water, the camera lingers on radiation burns — keloid scars — skin liquifying and falling off the bone — CUT TO EXT. Motel, Mojave — a yellow neon arrow with burnt-out bulbs — a barren parking lot through waves of heat — an empty swimming pool scarred by earthquakes — an air-conditioning unit chants its mantra as it leaks water that disappears in the sun. A door opens and the former actor exits, wearing a crumpled suit and carrying an empty briefcase. He's blinded by the light — CLOSEUP ON cringing eyelids DISSOLVING into a desert highway — a speeding car slips past in dust and there's nothing but emptiness ahead.

Been down *soo long…*

The former actor walks south along the cracked highway. Joshua trees act as sentinels, their hands raised to the sky prophesying doom to travelers who dare to travel these crumbling roads that are slowly being consumed by the dust. The former actor drifts into SLOW DISSOLVES of himself kicking rocks and baking in the sun.

Nooobody knows you when you're…

CLOSEUP on a hitchhiker's thumb conjuring a brand new black Imperial that crunches to a halt on the side of the road. The passenger door swings open and the red doughy face of the man in the gray flannel suit peers out with an idiot grin.

Hop aboard son.

DISSOLVE TO INT. Imperial — the former actor sweats shotgun next to the man in the gray flannel suit who grips the wheel with maniacal zeal.

Hot enough for you son? If you open up that glovebox, you might find a bit of relief.

The former actor opens the glove box and pulls out an unopened pint of Old Grand-Dad. A wink and a nod from the man in the gray flannel suit opens the bottle and they each take a long pull.

Ahhhhhhhh. That is a lifesaver, is it not? Now son, where you headed?

SIGH — L.A. I guess.

Tinseltown! Well, you are in luck son, because that is exactly my destination as well — though not for long — thank the lord. Don't get me wrong, it's a lovely city but there's no future there, not for you, not for me or for anyone.

CLOSEUP ON manic eyes and a salesman's rictus.

Now son, I know we've only known each other for going on a few minutes but may I be so bold as to give you some advice?

PAUSE — Sure.

Go East young man! You heard me correct — *East*! I know, I know, it sounds crazy. West! West! West! You heard it all your life, haven't you son? Go West, the future is out there, get discovered, and make it big. Well to that I say — *the West*?! *PFFFTTTT*! Everything out here's been *seen*! Everything out here's been *done*! Nothing out here to *explore*! Nothing to *conquer*! All gone! All exhausted! All used up. The territories are settled and the mines have all run dry. *The West*! There's no American Dream out here boy, for that you need to turn your narrow ass around and head back the other way. Away from the dried-up and sunken cities of the old frontier. *The future is in the East*! Now I know what you're thinking. *Back there*?! You mean the rotten and rusted cities of our Forefathers? *PFFFTTTT*! Abandoned you ol' coot! Abandoned long ago! And to that, I say *YES*! That's exactly what I'm talking about! The burnt out and hollow centers of Ford and Bethlehem, of Kodak and Chevy — no man's lands of rubble and urban decay...and all ripe for the taking! *Redevelopment*! *Revitalization*! *Renewal*! *Return*! It's the new frontier in the backyard of the old one and it is going fast. Why just last week I was right back there in Baltimore for a front-row seat to the birth of a new nation — FLASHBACK — NIGHT — EXT. City skyline in flames — a reptile, the size of which you would not believe, rose out of the bay and began to destroy everything as if it were a model. Every sweep of its hands, every swish of its tail, and every thundering footfall swept whatever remained of the husk of that so-called metropolis away and into extinction — and there I was, on the roof of the Belvedere Hotel as that scaly behemoth reared up and sang it's apocalyptic roentgen chatter on the entirety of the riverfront houses, surrounded by developers lighting cigars and cheering. Easier than evictions and more entertaining, they said. They got the privilege of watching it all burn and explode their portfolios while the ice melted around the champagne and dead fish washed up on the shore.

In that heady atmosphere — *my god*, you could see it all out before you — the burning bodies and buildings turning to ash before the glow of the sun on the horizon and the new dawn bringing with it, sparkling new shopping centers and condominiums — a new world rising out of the grave of the old — END FLASHBACK — It was beautiful. It was glorious and it could all be yours' son. All you have to do is get yourself a fast horse and hightail it in the opposite direction. Youngstown is just waiting to be re-discovered. *Hell son*, you could ride into any ghost town in the Midwest and I guarantee you, there will be an unknown valley, one in which you descend and discover an abandoned pit mine at its center, its mysteries long ago hollowed out and shipped off to be built into the traffic jam of today. There you'll find primitive people who worship the abandoned mines and factories. A cargo cult who dance and beat rhythms to attract Man F. Actor back to them, to give them purpose — and they'll be easy pickings. You can set yourself up as king in the primitive wastes. Your own kingdom to develop and rule over. I'm not lying. Scouts honor. They are all out there just waiting for you. Waiting like rubes for you to turn them into money. Do you think that you are the type of man who can do that? *Are you*? Or are you just going to sit there and give me that look?

What look is that?

That look that says I'm bullshitting you. That I'm some sort of huckster selling you a pie in the sky. Well, I swear to my ever-loving lord that I am not trying to flim-flam you. Hand on the good book, I am not a confidence man. What I'm telling you is the god's honest truth. Believe me — PAUSE — you know, I'll prove it to you.

The man in the gray flannel suit reaches over and flips on the radio to the tune of static. He twists the knob until a trusty narrator's voice is heard.

V.O. X-Day — It is now H-Hour plus 59 minutes. Operation Plowshare is in full effect. The United States Air Force has dropped multiple 40 kiloton warheads on the new territory of Greenland. This has had the effect of melting permafrost and more importantly creating the one thing they don't make anymore — *Land*! Real estate, new suburbs, shopping districts, restaurants, golf courses, and resorts!

You see son? It's inevitable — PAUSE — you hear me? Son? You asleep?

CUT TO eyelids drooping — highway lines merging with a FLASHBACK to a Pacific Island and the heat of a flame thrower pulling screams out of a hole in the ground — smell of burnt flesh wafts out on the soundtrack — FLASHFORWARD to the sewers of Los Angeles with the quavering fire engulfing giant ants controlled by stagehands — BEGIN DREAM SEQUENCE.

The flash took me by surprise.

EXT. The surface of the Sun SUPERIMPOSED on the South Pacific.

I shielded my eyes only to catch a glimpse of the bones in my hands.

Afterimage of Eniwetok floating in negative — the molten electrical buzz of insects — SLOW MOTION FADE to white — EXT. A fog-shrouded isle of the dead soundtracked by ominous bass notes.

I washed up on an alien shore days, maybe weeks later, half alive and with no face. Nothing more than a ragged blank spot, an empty vessel, once occupied by a nuclear scientist. I sat waterlogged on the beach to get my bearings but my thoughts began to fade in and out like radio signals drifting across the dial. Down the shore, there was the wrecked hull of a trawler and the fuselage of a Warhawk buried in the sand — burnt Quonset huts and the charred bones of lab animals — spent shells from automatic weapons fire — and a line of crooked wooden crosses beating a path into the jungle. I picked myself up and began to explore. The island was dense with brush and tangles of liana. Littered along the rough path were star maps and broken neon signs. As I walked under a grove of palms, I looked up to find the wreck of the USS Arkansas perched in the tops of the trees as if blown there by some great cataclysm. Silent and singed, it said nothing, so I pressed on into the interior. There I found a colonial mansion wallpapered with vines — the windows broke out — the doors off their hinges — the mattresses soaked with rainwater — bookshelves rotting with worm-eaten tomes — a patina of dust coated the globes and inkwells. In what was once a great study, dusty bones in a faded white suit sat in a rattan chair. CLOSEUP ON a note under a scotch glass — NO SIGN OF BOAT IN WEEKS — I FEAR NO RESCUE IS IMMINENT — I DO NOT WANT TO BE LEFT BEHIND. The florid script was the penmanship of a true gentleman. I looked into those empty eye sockets and I just thought — he must've had it all figured out. I dressed in his clothes and walked the halls and grounds of his plantation, gradually acquiring his face and mannerisms. His memories came to me in a slow trickle, filling my mind like an empty cup. I remembered the lab in the basement — equipment smashed — files in ash — the formerly great workspace of a great man. *I was a great man.* I had been A MAD DOCTOR on a tropical island — pathologist — researcher — astral wanderer — vivisectionist — surgeon — mass murderer. They threw me away but I showed them — the fools — the primitive beasts — EXTERMINATE THE BRUTES. My face fills the screen and cities burn inside of me. Sides of buildings fall and flames erupt in swirls that consume and send newsreel crowds running in terror. Cowboys slaughter Indians with canned pop guns in long tracking shots that move across me and eventually slow into a frame-by-frame death crawl. You can see my signal, blue and flickering in the CLOSEUP of the gun barrel smoking. I have become the destroyer, flickering through static on the dead television. Static FADES OUT to THE ECCENTRIC BILLIONAIRE as he watches the spy movie for the 130th time — INT. Hotel room at The Desert Inn — he sits in the dark, lit only by the B movie on a constant loop and the lights of the Strip flashing through the curtains. His appearance is that of a ragged beggar — A SERIES

OF CLOSEUPS on long brittle hair, a bedraggled beard, and fingernails of an unnatural length — yet his skull has the shape of a man with razor-sharp business acumen. Company men in black turtlenecks and a uniformed officer stand guard in his shadow, empty Campbell's chicken soup cans and cartons of chocolate marshmallow ice cream lay at their feet.

You have your orders and I have mine.

The film breaks in the projector — a Graflex 16, nothing but the best — and the eccentric billionaire throws a tantrum, spilling bottles of urine in the cavernous hotel room.

Get me the local affiliate I own!

CUT TO an Indian chief droning after midnight.

V.O. We interrupt this regularly scheduled program for a special broadcast.

FADE IN to Lyndon Johnson staring mute from the wall — INT. Institutional gray office — a flag lazily droops in the corner as men in suits meet to map out the future.

Gentlemen, we must not lose the suburbs, they are our last redoubt. The shelter from the nuclear storm. The landscape of our possible year zero. It must not be defiled, contaminated or god forbid written off. The stage set of our becoming must be ready for our walk on.

A smoldering Chesterfield curls rings of mellow flavor and nicotine incense into the office space, punctuating the reverence for authority in the presence of the sacred symbols — SERIES OF SHOTS — the president — the flag — a leather-bound bible — the capitol building as a matte painting outside the window.

Gentlemen, I do not need to tell you that this is a serious matter in need of serious discussion, so let us adjourn now to our den.

CUT TO INT. The Babylon Working, a hang out for aerospace employees and defense contractors — the camera moves past rowdy engineers groping dancers to the men in suits, drunk and backslapping each other in the red light of the strip club. The band pounds out a greasy burlesque as a plot drunkenly comes together between bouts of grab ass and ejaculations in slacks.

What won't we do to preserve this?

The needle skips and the music stops as new men, hollow men, faceless in dark suits interrupt the bacchanalia. They enter in SLOW MOTION, one at a time, until they form a wall of banal malevolence.

Gentleman, may I introduce MR. LOCKHEED, MR. DOUGLAS, MR. MARTIN, MR. BELL.

CUT TO AERIAL SHOT of a printed circuit board — INT. backseat — a man in a brown suit with lacquered hair sits in the back seat of a Lincoln Continental. A reel to reel recorder sits on his lap speaking the dry monotone of the eccentric billionaire as the Continental com-fortably rides the sleepy drift of the freeway.

V.O. The ideal agent for this mission must be exactly 6 feet tall — not 5 foot 9 or 6 foot 1 — 6 foot period. Ideal height for a man. He can look other men in the eye and look down on a love interest — do make a note there will be a separate voice memo about her forthcoming. He will have a slim yet athletic build, 170 pounds tops. Fit but not strong — can't be Superman — he's got to look like he's fit enough to where someone is going to believe that he's got no problem throwing some effete armchair commie across a room or holding his own with some hired kraut goon. Hair must be black and naturally perfect — he may use a little pomade but I'm talking like less than a teaspoon — I don't want a shining helmet on his head. No moles. No freckles. No scars. Handsome like an actor. Now, his most important features have to be his eyes and mouth — cold blue eyes and a cruel mouth. I can't stress this enough — cold eyes — cruel mouth. He's seen it all and sneered at it. As a representative of The United States and this company, even if he is covert, he must maintain a sense of superiority in all situations. This must be a priority, for the objective of this mission is to safeguard American interests abroad. This world is not big enough for the both of us — and by both of us, I mean us and them. If anybody is going to dictate the direction of this planet it is going to be us.

A jet engine roars offscreen — OPEN ON an unidentified foreign country. State police laden in heavy accents, speed through tiny old world streets chasing THE SECRET AGENT. His velocity is chrome and plastic, leaving old world elegance in the dust. On the seat next to him is the chalice with the false bottom containing the footage of the Soviet escape plan. His engine roar cracks the filigree and plaster — CLOSEUP ON his cold blue eyes in the rearview mirror — the foreign cops coming up fast — CLOSEUP ON the agent's cruel mouth turning upward into a deadly smirk causing the pursuit car to explode into flames. The agent careens around a corner and crashes the gate of Burbank airport, jumps from his car into a smooth gait, straights his suit, and dusts the dying continent from his shoulders. He boards a Pan Am plane outfitted with a spaced-out martini lounge and settles in for home.

Almost didn't get out of this one alive.

He hands the chalice over to THE CIA CHIEF who examines the footage frame by frame.

This will get us the jump we need on the Reds. Help us cripple their program. If anybody is going to escape this world, it will be *America first*. Your country owes you a debt of gratitude.

Not at all — already tanked and slurring violently — *iz mah job*.

Well, I have another one for you kid. A big one this time — they're threatening to destroy Topeka.

CUT TO EXT. A streamlined airport terminal.

THE NOTED SCIENTIST, recently returned from the jungles of Peru without his wife or trusty assistant — rumor has it he found them both caught in the midst of fever and delivered the final shot himself — arrives with a briefcase containing the fruits of ten years worth of research, now destined for the money men of upper Manhattan. Fellow travelers and bearded college professors playing out the pages of secret agent pulps watch and wait for their chance. The limousine pulls up curbside — CLOSEUP of the scientist's hand gripping the handle of his briefcase — the chauffeur opens the passenger door and the Reds rush the scientist — CLOSEUP on the hypodermic penetrating his neck — the noted scientist is pushed into the backseat and the limousine speeds away.

V.O. Now the briefcase needs to be quality. A name brand like Samsonite. It should be black leather with a dual combination lock. It has to look like it's carrying something important. What's actually in it doesn't matter. The briefcase is just one of those...*uhhh* what do they call them? A *uhhhh*...any of you guys know what I'm talking about? It's a plot device that moves the story along but doesn't actually matter? There's a name for it.

MUFFLED — Macguffin.

What?!

MUFFLED — Macguffin, sir.

Yes! *A MacGuffin!* That's it! The briefcase is a MacGuffin. You deserve a raise. Which reminds me — *sidenote* — Noah, I'm going to need you to go over the figures on my personal accounts again because someone must have put a comma or decimal in the wrong place — that balance can't be correct.

EXT. Island in the Florida Keys — crystal blue waters and lush vegetation — a picture-perfect paradise that hides a meeting of capitalists in Lincoln Continentals and exiled Cubans under dark palms. Company men and generals smoke gifted cigars with gusto, puffing out great clouds that obscure fascist smiles. The Cubans in unaffiliated olive drab, cast suspicion like shadows. They quickly talk amongst themselves, nodding eventually in consensus. A Cuban with the stripes of a Lieutenant opens the trunk of a brand-new Chevy and removes the briefcase. A company man with glasses and crew cut throws his cigar down and snaps his fingers. A three-star general opens the suicide doors of one of the Continentals and a generic man in a suit steps out with another briefcase handcuffed to his wrist. A second company man with a crew cut and glasses — they're interchangeable — unlocks the handcuffs and briefcases are exchanged as rifle shots ring out on the soundtrack — CUT TO frames 312 through 320 of an 8MM film — SLOW MOTION frame by frame of a political assassination in rush hour traffic — BACK AND TO THE LEFT — FLASHFORWARD to 1983 — Alamogordo, New Mexico — INT. Retirement home — THE DYING ASSASSIN sits before the camera, smoking Pall Malls with an oxygen machine hissing life into his skeleton.

Of course, I killed him. Ya act like it's some big deal or somethin'. I killed *lotsa* guys in those days. All for freedom and — COUGH — *uhhh* — COUGH — blood...or soil or whatever they used to say. Made no difference to me. They say get this guy and I go get 'em. He ain't gonna be squawking no more. Come walking behind 'em at the train station with a gun underneath the newspaper — POP — not a sound amid all that commerce. Afternoon commutes and ad copy made more noise than I did. Gotta lotta blood on my hands but I don't let it bother me. It was all just like when I was in business. Cold, cutthroat, and two-faced. Killing a guy is just like denying a guy a promotion. You know, sorry pal, you ain't goin' *nowhere* — chuckling that leads to a blood-spewing COUGH — LONG PAUSE — I ain't evil or anything. For me, it was a job. That's it. Had to put my kids through school.

Topeka must be protected at all costs.

V.O. An enemy agent comes in many disguises. Why, he could be the neighbor — or the local electrician — or maybe even that innocent looking bagboy at the grocery store. The enemy wears a mask molded for the everyday so that he may blend in and remain undetected by the very society he — or sometimes *she* — aims to undermine. They are an insidious and ingenious lot. That is why I want to make one thing very clear — I do not want any punches pulled on this thing. No punches pulled. Take the gloves off and really sock them in the mouth.

EXT. Train depot in the middle of nowhere.

He comes in on the South Pacific in the dead of night, looking sharp in a Panama hat and white suit. A walking black void where a soul should be. Handcuffed to his wrist is a briefcase bursting with money. Pulling out of the depot, the train lets out a lonely whistle that gets caught in his gravity and slides down an endless tunnel, reverberating into nothing. No light escapes from him. He walks under overpasses recruiting hobos and desperate escapees from chain gangs — secret meetings are arranged in church basements with segregationist sheriffs — ads are placed in the backs of men's magazines for those seeking adventure and purpose. Soon trucks appear on back highways hauling loads of hollow men — small, low flying aircraft touch down on makeshift runways — tent cities sprout on the properties of old plantations.

V.O. Each man will be issued the following: Three pairs of anonymous green fatigues, one pair of hobnail boots, one tactical belt, one combat knife, one mess kit, one entrenching tool, one first aid kit, one combat pack, and most importantly of all — one 6.5 x 52mm Mannlicher-Carcano Model 91/38.

Drills are conducted on sets made to resemble local supermarkets.

V.O. Vigorous combat patrolling creates constant pressure on irregular forces. This keeps the guerrillas and the population that maintains them on the move, it disrupts their security and organization, weakens them physically, destroys their morale, and denies them the opportunity to conduct operations.

Rifle shots ring out on a continuous loop from an abandoned drive-in converted to a firing range. Target practice is carried out on cardboard blow-ups from *Look* and *Life*.

V.O. Upon encountering friendly elements the following specific factors should be considered: 1. The motivation and loyalties of various segments of the population in the area. 2. The vulnerability of friendly or potentially friendly elements to coercion by terror tactics and their susceptibility to enemy and friendly propaganda. Particular attention should be given to non-homeowners, small business owners, elementary through high school teachers, union members, and non-denominational Christians.

Manuals on hand-to-hand combat and guerilla warfare are burned after reading. CUT TO the general entering stage right wrapped in the stars and stripes.

There are a hundred more training camps just like this, hidden all over the country. Men just like you, all willing to put their lives on the line for the values we share. Face the flag. See what's written there? The history, the progress, and the heritage we share. I don't know about you, but I'll be damned if I'm going to let some commie fuck rip *that* down. 'Cause they will. You give 'em a chance and they will. You let them park their asses right off our coast — close enough for them to breathe that red fog right onto our shores — *and they will*. And when they do, we're not going to have time to prepare like we're doing right now. No. It'll happen like that — SNAPS — overnight. We'll be surrounded. We ain't going to be John Wayne storming the shores of Iwo Jima. No sir, we'll be lucky if we get to be Henry Fonda in that last scene from *Fort Apache* — standing tall and firm under wave after wave of Apaches — CLOSEUP on a pistol in a white-gloved hand firing studio blanks — shooting till the last bullet — fighting a doomed battle — and ultimately falling with grace and dignity. You know, when I saw that movie, I just sat there dumbfounded. The end title came up and the credits rolled and I just sat there because I couldn't believe what I had just seen. It had been a vision of the future. A full-fledged prophetic message beamed onto the screen and projected right into me. That's what I saw. An America about to be swallowed under the waves. And I pledged right then and there to do something about it. I aim to fight the future gentlemen.

The general walks off stage to ghost-ridden silence. Faceless men dissolve into petro-chemical exhaust and barking police dogs. Fleets of phantom ships anchor offshore. A B-26 makes leaflet drops of *Better Homes and Gardens* and *Sears* catalogs. Shortwave radio stations broad-casting from unknown locations change format from rock & roll to coded messages and brimstone spewing preachers. Regularly scheduled program-ming is interrupted by transmissions that look like slick commercials advertising the message — RESIST AND YOU WILL PERISH.

V.O. We now return you to our regularly scheduled program.

TRACKING SHOT over the beach before light. Sunken dead eyes appear in the sky. A water-logged copy of *Good Housekeeping* washes up onshore. A flash in the sky far to the west and men in rubber suits rise out of the surf — slick wet with fossilized crude — they lumber forward, staring blankly with ping-pong ball eyes and breathing heavy stalking breaths through slimy suction-cup mouths. They leave trails that shimmer with petroleum rainbows as they hunt under early morning street lamps. The insistent organ of an abandoned church begins its steady foreboding drone. A woman screams. Terror radiates off her in trembling waves that distort reality itself — putting every-thing out of sorts and unable to be shifted back together. A dark presence rises and drifts forward as a gun fires in CLOSEUP — and she still screams as roving death squads roll silently with the weight of Panzer divisions through the streets — the fog rolls in — people disappear in the shadows of parking lots — hotels out on desert highways are rented out as makeshift interrogation centers — empty swimming pools overflow with executions — endless firing squads chamber fresh rounds — CLOSEUP on the smoking barrel of a rifle.

FIRE!

CUT TO INT. The kitchen in the home of the future — the place where tomorrow meets today — push-button magic by frigidaire. Mom busies herself with convenience as Dad sips his coffee.

How could such a pretty wife make such *bad* coffee?

AUDIENCE LAUGHS.

I'm sorry dear.

Just do better. That's all I ask.

AUDIENCE LAUGHS. Enter the son. AUDIENCE CHEERS. He throws his baseball and mitt on the table and sits next to Dad, beaming as THE ALL-AMERICAN BOY.

Morning pop!

And how is my little slugger today?

CLOSEUP of dad's fist giving his son a fake belt on the chin.

Gosh, pop — his smile turns to a frown — everything is the pits today. *First*, I woke up this morning and found Sparky dead. He was just a pile of bones like something had ate him right up. *Then*, I went all the way out to the ballfield just to find out my game was canceled. *Everything is just the pits*.

AUDIENCE SIGHS — Dad takes the pipe from out of his mouth.

Oh don't worry son, I'm sure things are going to turn around.

I don't know pop — the boy's face suddenly grim — there's some strange stuff happening out there. Pretty sure I saw smoke out on the edge of town.

Dad puts a reassuring arm around the boy's shoulders.

I know that whatever is happening out there *seems* scary but really son, we have nothing to worry about. You see, this great nation is made for men like you and me — WIDESHOT of American plenty rolling over their faces — and somewhere out there are men just like us, putting their lives on the line so that we can enjoy the fruits of this magnificent country. They are out there doing the unimaginable — *the unthinkable* — *the unconscionable* — so that our way of life can continue. These things have to be done.

AUDIENCE CLAPS AND CHEERS as the kitchen set splinters and armed men in green fatigues storm the studio.

Now just a minute! What is the meani—

Dad is cut off as one of the men smashes him square with a rifle butt — CLOSEUP of his face exploding into a fountain of blood — AUDIENCE SCREAMS.

V.O. We'll be right back after this commercial break. Don't go anywhere.

INT. Remnants of the kitchen set. One of the three walls has been torn down revealing its plywood backing. Dad lays in a fetal position, swallowing blood and broken teeth. Mom and Son have their hands and feet tied. Mom screams with a boot in her back while the boy lays face down with a gash on the side of his head, bleeding into his eyes. The audience continues to shriek as they are rounded up by the group of armed men — hard faceless men armed to the teeth — they speak in barks and gunshots — they trample everything with their boots and leave hot glowing trails of an unknown substance in their wake. The cameras begin to swivel violently and lose their framing — SORRY, WE ARE EXPERIENCING TECHNICAL DIFFICULTIES — EXT. Main street, now an alien planet. A landscape trans-formed by the smoke of burning garbage. Tanks and armored personnel carriers roll through the avenues, crushing cars and broadcasting orders over loudspeakers.

STOP RESISTING. WE ARE BUILDING A BETTER WORLD.

CUT TO BREAKING NEWS — Information is still sketchy but what we do know is that an American lead invasion force has invaded America to prevent further Communist infiltration. The death toll at this point is unknown. We go live to our man on the scene. Jim, what can you tell us?

EXT. Suburban neighborhood. A camera-ready face stands in front of a line of middle-class citizens stumbling by with their hands behind their heads.

Well, Jim, we are here in Kalamazoo where a forced death march of homeowners is underway. We are going to try to see if we can get a statement from one of the participants. Maam, do you know where you are going? Miss? Miss? Do you know who these men are or what they are doing?

A frantic woman with blood running out of her ears looks directly into the camera.

I don't get it! What is this?! *Why is this happening to us*?! I voted for Eisenhower and Nixon! I hate Communists and coloreds just like everyone else — Why are they doing this to us? *They're not hurting the right people*!

CUT TO INT. The conference hall of the Sheraton Suites. Suburbanites wait bound and blindfolded as shots ring out. Mom and dad shiver against the wall while faceless men stand guard over a hushed whimper.

FIRE!

GUNSHOTS — the emergency exit bursts open. The firing squad enters and begins grabbing the collected suburbanites at random. Screams erupt and fear ripples through the room like a physical wave. Mom and dad are dragged outside and lined up with the rest of the condemned next to the dumpsters. In front of them is THE HEAD OF THE CHAMBER OF COMMERCE mumbling excuses and prayers.

This can't be happening...God...can't be happening...what didn't I do…

CLOSEUP on dad's hands slowly working their way free. The Head of the Chamber of Commerce

continues to mumble as the line is forced forward
toward the execution area.

FIRE!

GUNSHOTS — EXT. The rear or the Sheraton
Suites. A blindfolded car salesman stands
shaking in front of a wall pocked and crumbling
from bullets. The firing squad stands silent
before him waiting for the signal. The camera
pans over from these faceless men to a stack
of bleeding corpses where the reclining CIA
chief, a man in a rubber suit — his cheap eyes
rolling up under heavy lids — his breath labored
and reeking of blood — raises a slime drenched
tentacle like a drunk patrician.

Ready.

The firing squad takes aim. CLOSEUP on the
car salesman cowering — the CIA chief's tentacle
listlessly slaps down upon his engorged belly.

FIRE!

GUNSHOTS — the car salesman hits the wall and
crumples to the ground — the CIA chief lets a
loud sigh — CLOSEUP on the trail of blood as
the car salesman is dragged over to the stack of
corpses — the CIA chief raises his tentacle and
makes a sleepy gesture. The Head of the Chamber
of Commerce is pushed in front of the wall.

No! No! No...you can't...*you can't do this!
It's not right!*

Right?

CLOSEUP on the CIA chief as his suction cup mouth lets out a bemused laugh — SLOW ZOOM into his monstrous face.

Right? Who are you to speak to me about right or wrong? I will have you know that I am a parson's son, brought up a Presbertyian. My morality has never been a question. Yes, I have directed men to kill — to strangle, stab, shoot, poison, burn, and disintegrate. I have overseen the assassination of children, raised phantom air forces, and overthrown governments for the sake of banana sales. Yes, I have done these things but my *morality* is not a subject of debate. All these things I have carried out have been done with the most crystalline of intentions. We must do these things. They serve a higher purpose.

The CIA chief raises his tentacle.

Ready.

CLOSEUP on dad's hands loose and waiting for the right moment.

FIRE!

GUNSHOTS — dad grabs mom and makes a break for the tree line — volleys of rifle fire are heard as they crash through the vegetation and run breathless through blue flickering television films of ruined cities with empty streets, wrecked cars, and swirling trash — they escape into increasingly dead roads and empty towns — freezing winds blow in from the north and the sky fills with snow and emptiness.

V.O. Will they survive in this brutal and inhospitable land? Can they escape this new world?

INT. UNITED STATES

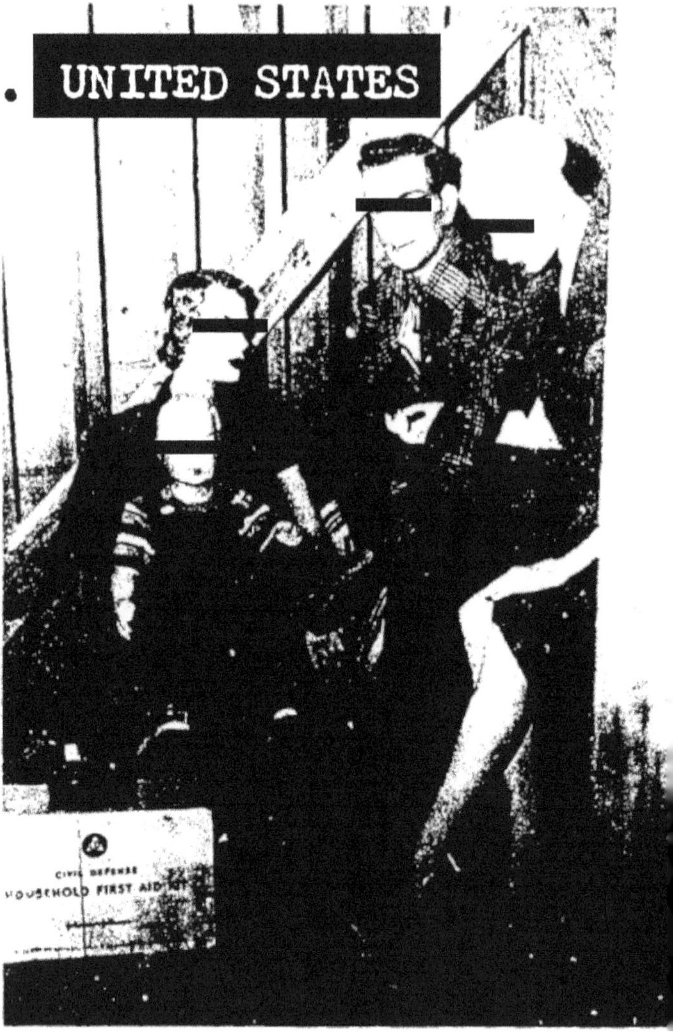

Scene 19—Basement corner room at 7500 ft after blast.

UNCLASSIFIED

~~CONFIDENTIAL — RESTRICTED DATA~~

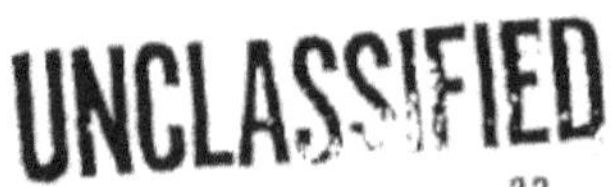

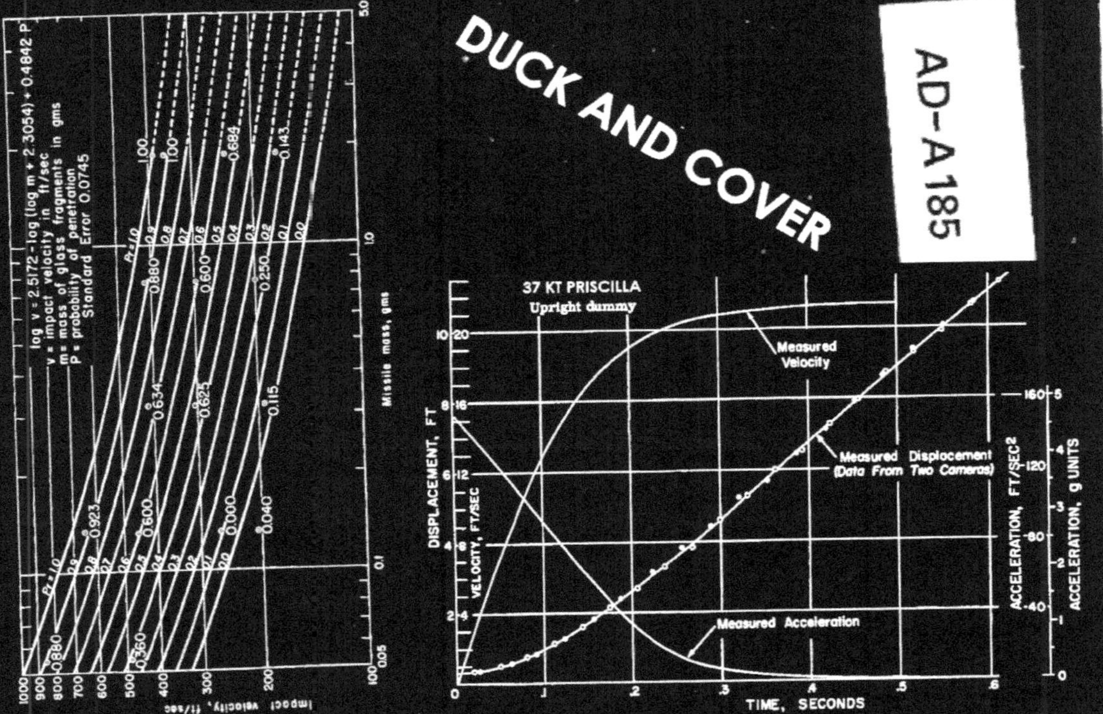

DUCK AND COVER
AD-A185
Probability of penetration of glass fragments into the abdomen   Fig. 41
log v = 2.5172 - log (log m + 2.3054) + 0.4842 P
v = impact velocity in ft/sec
m = mass of glass fragments in gms
P = probability of penetration
Standard Error 0.0745
Missile mass, gms
Impact velocity, ft/sec
P = 1.0
37 KT PRISCILLA
Upright dummy
Measured Velocity
Measured Displacement (Data From Two Cameras)
Measured Acceleration
DISPLACEMENT, FT
VELOCITY, FT/SEC
ACCELERATION, FT/SEC2
ACCELERATION, g UNITS
TIME, SECONDS

.IVING WITH NUCLEAR WEAPONS

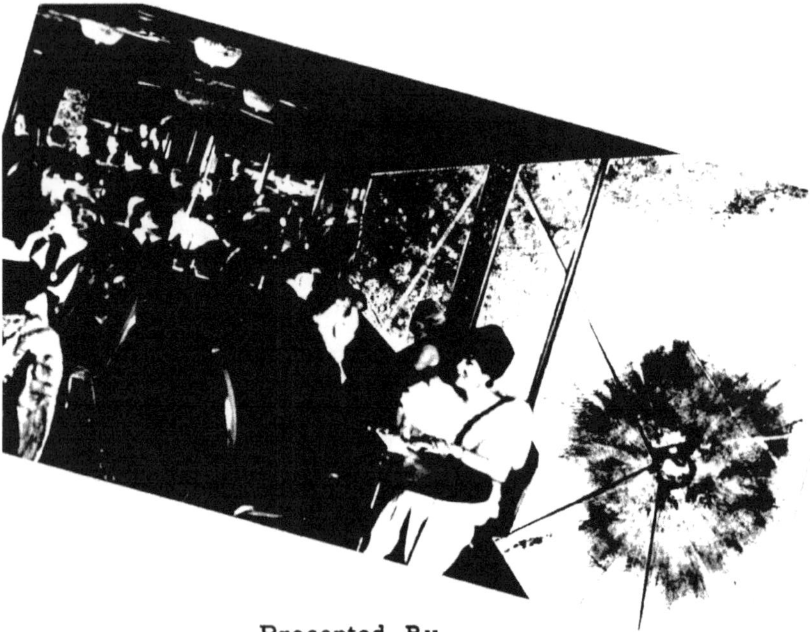

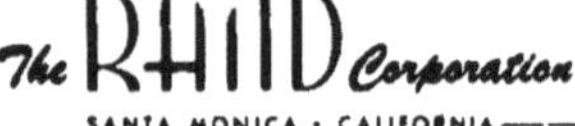

Presented By

The RAND Corporation

SANTA MONICA · CALIFORNIA

A Monster Movie

EXT. The beach at low tide, haunted by silence — EXT. The cave at Bronson Canyon teleported through editing onto the shore. Inside a million flesh-eating crabs skitter over each other to pick bones clean. Giant inhuman eyes lay sleeping in the depths. The cave exhales a fetid breath as it dreams nightmares decades into the future. Back on the beach, the air turns foul with the stench of death and the heavy taste of burnt plastic — WIDE SHOT of the beach in 16mm and the monster stalks the sands. The thick green rubber of his suit is shredded and dragging after him like the train of a diseased monarch. He shambles across the sand making a trail with limbs crusted black with blood. Weaving in and out of the palms, he searches for the answer. A 50 kiloton pain reverberates down an empty hospital hall in his head, bursting out through his eardrums. Breathing labored and hot through the minuscule slits in his mask, he tears through vegetation that turns to smoke and the monster is center stage at the magician's late-night cocktail act.

Gentleman, THE GREAT KAHN!

INT. The RAND Lounge — cigarette smoke and applause rise into the cloistered air as the top-hatted occultist takes a bow. The best and the brightest are all here — thermonuclear mandarins — Chicago School economists — Ivy League doomsayers — egghead war mongers — punch card programmers — second strike zealots — Brylcreem statisticians — well-bred boys, kicking their heels up and cutting loose.

Mr. Lockheed, Mr. Douglas, Mr. Martin, Mr Bell, your table is ready.

The Great Kahn throws his hands into the air calling for silence.

And for my next illusion, I shall go beyond the unthinkable! Gentlemen, prepare yourselves for the inevitable.

The spell begins with incantations to gods both ancient and new — arcane words and game theory — CLOSEUP of hands curling in wide-eyed tension — the lights dim and the film runs backward.

You will begin to count in reverse...100..99 ..98..97...95....3 — 2 — FILM START—

F.I.T. T.V. STUDIO

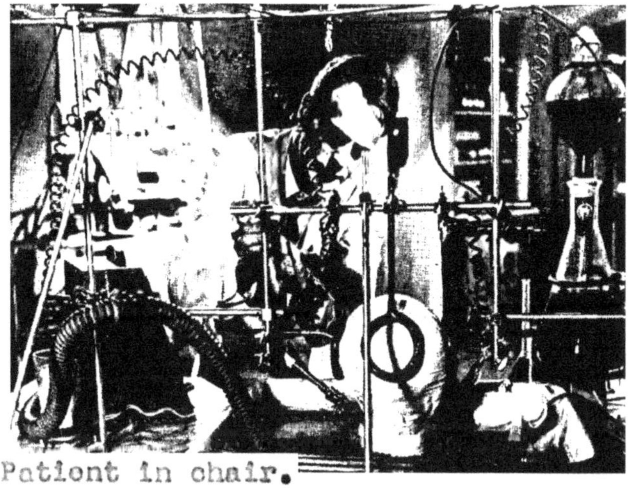

Patient in chair.

Doctor and 2 TV cameras

INT. NIGHT - MEDIUM SHOT - dream
CLOSE SHOT - nightm

It Came From Bikini Atoll

CUT TO EXT. Texaco station — NIGHT — a beat-up Mercury sits next to the gas pump while the owner pays inside. CLOSEUP ON the keys still in the ignition. Mom and dad peek out from around the corner. CLOSEUP ON their unwashed faces as they nod to each other. They make a dash for the car, throw open its doors and scramble inside. CLOSEUP OF tire tread spitting dirt. CUT TO mom and dad cruising away towards a new beginning, breathing a sigh of relief.

Don't worry, it's over now.

CUT TO the blinding flash of oncoming head-lights — tail fins flying around deadly curves — winding roads unsafe at any speed — glass bursting in a shower of crystal pain and chrome dismemberment — twisted and broken, the film leader runs out to black then unspools on the floor leaving only a luminous white — CUE the black Cadillac. THE EX-NAZI SCIENTIST arrives on the scene as the wrecked car begins to burn. The camera becomes the eyes of THE DYING

HOUSEWIFE looking out through burning fenders and broken windows. A shaking hand reaches in and pulls her body from the wreck — CUT TO EXT. A trailer rotting amid Spanish Moss in Huntsville, Alabama. The black Cadillac pulls up slow and paranoid, coming to a halt in front of the decrepit trailer. The driver-side door opens and we CUT TO A MEDIUM SHOT of the ex-Nazi scientist who stares across the roof of his car into a FLASHBACK of OFFSCREEN screams that become transcripts in the hands of Air Force generals.

Don't worry doc. You're playing on the right team now.

BACK TO PRESENT DAY — the ex-Nazi scientist slams the car door with resolve and marches to the rear of the car to open the trunk. The camera takes the POV of the trunk and we see the ex-Nazi scientist from below, bathed in an unholy light — CUT TO REVERSE SHOT and we see the broken body of THE DEAD HOUSEWIFE. He reaches in and begins the tedious task of carrying her body from the car to the trailer. As he drags her through the entrance of the trailer, the camera PANS UP to a sign just above the door — RESEARCH INSTITUTE FOR AVIATION MEDICINE — CUT TO black.

Are you awake? Can you see?

FADE IN and awaken in the laboratory smeared in the curvature of glass. INT. A computer lab. A SERIES OF SHOTS — tape machines spooling and printouts spilling onto the floor — a tarantula crawling through a web — a haunted house skeleton hanging from a painted brick wall — a psychic haze drifting through passageways — blood crawling down wallpaper. The soundtrack echoes with screams, the howls of moonlit hounds, the creaking of rotting doors, and the clanking of chains.

Can you hear me? Are you conscious of your surroundings?

The camera focuses in on the distorted image of the ex-Nazi scientist in his white lab coat with the static of a giant cathode ray tube dancing behind him. The radio crackle of dying lungs crowds the frame.

I say again, *can you see?*

A woman's voice radiates slowly from a point OFFSCREEN, quiet and hollow as if trapped behind glass.

Fire...Burning...

Yes! Yes. That is quite good — the ex-Nazi scientist claps his hands in triumph — quite good.

Fire...Burning...

Yes. I hear you but that was from before, you understand? What you are describing is the crash. I'm very sorry but the fellow you were with did not make it. I did everything possible to save you...or I should say, I did everything possible to save your body. It unfortunately was too far gone. I had to save what I could.

You are a very lucky girl. If I had not come along when I did that would have been it for you, my dear. *Kaputt*. If it were not for my research...*my work*...you would be lost. So let us show a bit of gratitude and get back to the business at hand, shall we? *Yes*? Yes. Now I need you to look ahead, past the crash.

I see only black.

CLOSEUP of hands twisting dials, selecting channels, and fixing the vertical hold — tape reels spinning — a Tesla coil sparking — a slight adjustment of arcing rabbit ears. The electron beam of the giant cathode ray tube begins to sing its high stinging whine and faint signals appear on screen.

Now...what can you see?

The voice of the dead housewife comes in like a spectral vapor, enveloping everything in its broadcast and taking over the screen. FADE IN from black. INT. Suburban living room.

I see...I see myself in my home. I'm now played by a different actor. A younger woman with much lighter hair and a tragic face. She smokes and waits by the tv on her widow's watch. She can see the Apollo capsule floating in orbit around the moon with dead men inside. It's all in black and white like one of those old bad movies. She can see their frozen images smeared on the television screens of mission control standing in for in my living room, a tomb mold of frost and static obscuring their faces. I don't want to see these images, she says. She turns away to look out the window and up in the sky is a CUT TO the surface of the moon as an unbroken set with not a footprint in sight. No escape, she tells herself as she flips the channels and enters the land of the dead — TV movie adaptations of Southeast Asian quagmires starring THE DEAD NEIGHBOR BOY and countless unnamed extras that the viewers will never care to remember nor mourn — late-night broadcasts of men in suits burning cities down to heaps of cigarette ash — archival newsreels of fascists repurposed and spliced with new footage of Levittown death cult devotees screaming for renewal. It's all full of ghosts, she screams and tears off running into the night. She runs for years in the dark streets, breathing silent 1 AM fog until she comes to a desert motel on a distant planet and finds a room under the flashing sign, all the while polaroids yellow and television signals disperse out across the galaxies. EXT. Highway outside of Barstow. She is THE FADED STAR, cloaked in furs and dark shades, hiding out in a desert motel with stitches burning red. INT. Shitty hotel room — water stains on the ceiling — the smell of rotting carpet — the rustle of insect legs through the sheets — vomit congeals in the ice bucket — barbiturates blur into the carpet — vacant television lighting — DO NOT DISTURB — all calls held except for Hollywood. She fears that she will disappear in the light of day. She can feel it. The falling — space overlapping — another landscape, another time — drifting into shadows. CUT TO the air-conditioner droning its tears into the carpet — CUT TO THE ASTRONAUT'S

WIFE laying on the bathroom floor — CUT TO THE PILOT'S WIFE crying in the hall — CUT TO CLOSEUP on the face of the scientist's wife distorted in a slow-motion scream — CUT TO the beach before the end credits, watching and waiting for any sign of life. The room grows bright — CLOSEUP as she wakes up to find she is still herself. The room is lit by the blue shifting light of the television set and the pulse of neon through the curtains. She lays in bed among empty bottles, watching reruns with CLOSEUPS of glassy eyes. CUT TO INT. Hotel bathroom. CLOSEUP of the faucet running and the water swirling down the drain. She stares at herself in the mirror. The woman playing me has visibly aged and even she has trouble recognizing herself. She sees the harried face of the failed runaway, desperate to attain escape velocity and be rid of the wreckage piling up below — FLASHES of THE LOST ASTRONAUT adrift and helpless in the dark. I don't want to see these things. She bends over into the sink to wash but lets the water fall through her fingers. CLOSEUP of hands covering eyes with a pressure bent on transformation — the hands drop in SLOW MOTION as she looks into the mirror — and she becomes THE PILOT.

Helmet?

Check.

Oxygen mask?

Check.

Flight Suit?

Check.

Pilot needed on set.

Turning toward the door, she walks out of the bathroom and onto the harbor in WIDESHOT where the Pan Am Clipper sits docked in glorious sunshine — RUN OPENING CREDITS — TITLE CARD — THE AIR CONDITIONED EXOTICA. It stars the usual suspects, a ship of fools including THE SQUARE JAWED CO-PILOT, THE DRUNKEN HEIRESS, THE TEXAS OILMAN, THE NERVOUS INSURANCE AGENT, THE INNOCENT NEWLYWEDS, and the atomic scientist. They all take their seats as the flight crew readies for takeoff. SERIES OF SHOTS — radial engines cough and propellers spin into life — gin and whiskey bottles are secured in the lounge area — radio dials hum — baggage hold secured — the four-star chef checks on the beef Wellington in the galley — white gloves inventory the silver and crystal — star charts are rolled and a gold sextant is placed in a velvet lined box — seatbelts are fastened — the co-pilot begins his log. He looks up and doffs his cap as the pilot enters the cockpit. She brings with her a dreamy atmosphere of SLOW MOTION gloss. Her stiff movements are out of sync with the action on set as she sleepwalks with a heavy-lidded gaze and a flat prerecorded voice that plays on a reel to reel OFFSCREEN.

Make ready for departure.

Ready for departure when you are captain.

She takes the controls and taxi's the clipper across the bay. The hull splits blue ocean glass until it glides into the air on a peal of brass and cascading harps. CUE *The Ritual of the Savage* — swirling flutes carry the wings upward toward perfect Technicolor skies as marimba strikes map a route through painted Madison Avenue clouds promising extraordinary and luxuriant phenomena in the heavens — mirages and castles in the sky — fata morgana of interplanetary structures — great columned buildings of violet and coral sunsets — martian palaces with exotic, scimitar wielding green guards and veiled princesses of Venus reclining in perpetual leisure. Rhythmic congas beat out rituals of incense smoke that curl into the wavering opulent figure of the pur-ple-skinned HIGH PRIESTESS who shimmies around stone gods like a coiling snake. Sophisticated alien savages bow before the altar. The high priestess leads a pageant of dancing Venusian girls and royal warriors bedecked in glittering native chants as shipwrecked astronauts peep from behind temple columns. Moonlit washes of strings carry the lost astronaut into the arms of the high priestess and they embrace under easy listening stars that shine in high fidelity into the dawn.

We will always be together, won't we?

DISSOLVE to the pilot in shadow against a cold sliver of blue light before daybreak. The rasp of her breath through the oxygen mask is heard on the soundtrack. CUT TO EXT. The dawn of time — the stars still visible before daylight — WIDESHOT of the dark Pacific with muted tribal drums anticipating the sun's slow ascent — CLOSEUP on the eyes of the atomic scientist, waking from an untroubled sleep. The atomic scientist stretches out in his seat and looks toward the window. He gazes out the porthole as the orchestra swells and golden fire fills the world. CUT TO the clipper soaring through creation — it makes a diving turn and below, in the glittering water, a volcano rises from the depths to spew molten rock that flows and steams for millennia before cooling into paradise. DISSOLVE into palm trees swaying in the sweet wind of morning.

Prepare for landing.

The clipper touches down just outside the lagoon — scratches on perfect crystal blue — and drifts into the sound of a busy port. The camera PANS across the water to reveal the arrivals backed up and waiting for hours to reach the dock.

Welcome to Rongelap.

Passengers disembark on the dock to a handshake from the square-jawed co-pilot and a garland of orchids from island girls in grass skirts.

We hope you enjoy your stay.

The pilot steps onto the rotting wood of the dock and watches as the empty clipper is towed into the middle of the lagoon and burned — CUT TO the tail section as it sinks down into the water to lay with the USS Arkansas, HIJMS Nagato, and the SS Venture to grow sea moss and rust in the aquatic boneyard.

There's no going back.

LONG TRACKING SHOT off the dock onto perfect white sands, shaded by palms and echoing with birdsong that is gradually replaced by the sound of the pilot's breathing. The camera stops on the quiet village TRANSFORMED into the bustling tourist stop. Where once there were sleepy rhythms and the atmosphere of creeping vines, there are now fully stocked gift shops, hotels, and casinos. FLASHBACK to THE SURVIVING OFFICER of the USS Saratoga drifting for days on the parched desert of the sea before washing ashore on a primitive world. To survive, he goes savage and joins the native tribe through trials of manhood and blood rituals. Using the power of positive thinking and advice gleaned from *Forbes* columns, he rises to become chief.

You pull yourself up by your bootstraps. What one can achieve through sheer force of will is unbelievable.

He reshapes the island society, melding noble savage and peak America into a winning business strategy that makes him a fortune, allowing him to spend his days decadent and degenerate on his throne, downing Mai Tai's and drowning in native women.

Where do we come from? What are we? Where are we going?

BACK TO PRESENT DAY — INT. Casino — an A-frame building of bamboo poles and rattan walls adorned with spears and tiki masks. Green baize topped tables spit cards and eat money to howls of delight as paychecks are fed into slot machines that crash and ring with the sound of pennies falling. Loaded dice land in piles of cigarette ash and stare snake eyes as cries erupt from the back of the gaming room. Tourists drunk and screaming look on in exotic wonder and disgust at the primal scene underway — babbling tongues across the radio in the cockpit — stained money flys back and forth by the fistful as two cocks tear and gouge at each other — CLOSEUP of fluttering wings and slashing spurs — blood stains white Panama suits. The birds lock their spurs into each other's throats and fall to the dust — the ring falls silent — the handlers enter and examine their fighters. The dead cocks' entrails are spilled out onto the dirt floor and all eyes reach in to divine the future — gizzards, wires, hearts, and solid-state parts speak in a language all will come to know and few will be able to speak.

The House wins.

As money is handed over in silence, the camera moves out the backdoor of the casino onto a bamboo bridge that connects the gaming house to the bar. Men in gray flannel suits vomit over the railing into jungle foliage and stumble back through the door under the sign — TRADER TIBBETTS' UP AND ATOM LOUNGE. INT. Tiki bar. The camera stops at the threshold and peers into the gloom to reveal a pile of bodies lying next to a wasted crowd of ad executives in Hawaiian attire, drinking in oblivious merriment among a passel of pigs rooting through a mud of blood and spilt drinks — Zombies, Blue Hawaiis, Navy

Grog, Test Pilots, Cobra Fangs and Singapore Slings in authentic native skulls with little umbrellas. The band in matching sailor suits sit in the corner vibrating smooth wavelengths that transport fresh sons of Madison Avenue into the bar via a watery shimmer that connects disparate frames. They arrive in loungewear, already sauced and jet-lagged from the edit — CLOSEUP on red-rimmed eyes soaked in martinis and back issues of Playboy — nostrils flaring with the smell of death and rum. The newcomers make a break for the bar, tripping over bodies and fighting the crowd to be served.

Hey Boy! One of those fancy drinks over here! *I earned it today*!

Against the far wall, at the bar's only table, sits THE OLD INDUSTRIALIST in his smoking jacket. His Chinese servant, a loyal man he rescued from the squalor of Shanghai, stands dutifully by his side with a tray and crystal decanter of scotch, occasionally refilling the old industrialist's glass as he rambles in his perfect mid-Atlantic accent to no one.

Have I told you of the time I nearly did not escape with my life from the jungles of darkest Africa? Dreadful time that — CLOSEUP as scotch dribbles off his chin and onto his velvet smoking jacket — Real exploring that. Not like these young Turks.

He points his cigar at the clamoring scions of Fifth avenue with their Exxon and 3M salaries sticking out of their back pockets.

Exploring, it is a lost art. Did I ever tell you of the time I had to put down a mutiny of those midnight bastards? Shot every one of them. *Dreadful time that.*

The old industrialist empties his glass and the servant refills it with deft precision.

Ahhh...I would give anything to set my eyes upon a virgin world again. Those were the days. The thrill of discovery. My good man, you really have no idea, there is nothing else quite like it — SIGH — like bringing fire to a dark world. *Prometheus in a pith helmet*! *Ha*! Yes — LONG PAUSE — quite like that I should say.

He drains his glass and peers through it like a spyglass.

The days of Prometheus.

POV through whiskey glass — SERIES OF SHOTS — stockpiles of ivory tusks — rubber trees bleeding — a pile of severed hands — blood slowly working into a stain on khaki — a landfill of tires that stretches to the horizon — clacking pool balls and the sprocket holes of celluloid whirring through the camera — the distant sounds of rifle shots and screams can be heard OFFSCREEN.

Gone like yesterday, my good man. Gone and forgotten.

CLOSEUP on sunken bloodshot eyes that partially DISSOLVE and remain DOUBLE EXPOSED over a factory building. EXT. Factory — a long-span building made of rusting sheet metal that radiates a blinding heat — the rhythmic violence of manufacturing can be heard on the soundtrack — CUT TO INT. Factory floor — a vast gloom and oppressive heat pervades the factory floor, lit only by furnaces melting sand — CLOSEUP on the sun screaming raw commerce — CUT TO molten glass extruded in long, thin ropes into black oil caked stamping machines that expel rough beads into great vats to be smoothed and polished — CLOSEUP on weathered hands grabbing handfuls of beads and setting them one-by-one under a drill press — CLOSEUP on a delicate feather brush painting a minuscule A on a glass bead — CUT TO wheelbarrows full of seashells dumping their contents into great piles — CUT TO the center of the factory floor where in the half-light of industry, Marshallese women sit and string beads and shells together into bracelets — CLOSEUP on bracelets that say AELON KEIN AD — SUBTITLES: OUR ISLANDS — CUT TO EXT. The Southdale Center made from bamboo, thatched roofs, and the remnants of a set leftover from a production of *South Pacific* — the tourists pour into the shops where they trade paychecks for trinkets — INT. The Bali Ha'i Store — low glass display cases filled with authentic jewelry.

Darling! That's perfect!

The shopgirl in the grass skirt pulls a bead and shell bracelet from the case and drapes it over a woman's elegant wrist.

It's so stylish and affordable. *Darling, please*?

The woman turns to her husband who smiles as they embrace and FREEZE FRAME into a magazine ad seen in dentist's office all over the U.S. CROSS DISSOLVE into streams of happy shoppers — the march of commerce — CLOSEUPS on bright happy smiles moving in the shade of the palms — the camera PANS up to reveal the wreck of the USS Gilliam perched in the tops of the trees as if blown there by some great cataclysm. CUT TO NIGHT. EXT. Beach — the tide is low and the sea appears as a massive black void that joins the stars — all sound is swallowed in this abyss. The camera stares down the long stretch of dark shoreline to find a single point of light that grows as it draws near. One light soon becomes many as a line of tourists march down the beach carrying tiki torches — CLOSEUPS on pale, hard faces with crew cuts and bouffants that DISSOLVE into screaming protesters throwing rocks at school children and smiling guards waving at departing trains — the line of tourists and torches file up the beach and disappear into a great lodge. INT. Elks Lodge. CUE the ritual of the savage — paeans to sinister white gods and diabolical ceremonies at torch-lit altars bathed in orgasmic red light and dead chickens. The Mystic Order of the Elks dance barefoot in rhythmic circles, playing out esoteric rites conducted by a LAWRENCE WELK LOOK-ALIKE, while incense and cigar smoke weave sacred atmo-spheres. THE HIGH PRIEST wears aviator sunglasses and beads over his face as he presides on high atop the hall stage, flanked by a big band in professional blue suits and conical hoods. THE HEAD OF THE ORANGE COUNTY BETTER BUSINESS

BUREAU sits offstage on his own platform as an exalted guest, his body draped in blood dark furs that drip over his Sunday suit — CLOSEUP on his forced smile as he bends down to whisper to his wife.

This is a *helluva* 4th of July parade. We'll do well to respect these people's customs. Savages like these are liable to become vicious.

CUT TO MEDIUM SHOT of the high priest as he throws his hands into the air and the music stops. Dancing tourists come to a halt and face the stage. The high priest rises and walks to a small podium to call the meeting to order — CLOSEUP on sunglasses in deep red, reflecting the light of a hundred tiki torches.

Hear me, brothers and sisters! We gather to honor our gods! We say their names!

The crowd answers — EISENHOWER — NIXON — GOLDWATER — LEMAY — WALKER — ROCKWELL — BIRCH — COUGHLIN — FORD — WAYNE!

Hear me, brothers and sisters! We serve at the behest of the secret chiefs! We say their names!

UNIVAC — BURROUGHS — IBM — HONEYWELL — CDC — NCR — HP!

And we gather brothers and sisters to say the sacred words — CLOSEUP ON the high priest's mouth as he releases a whisper — not in my backyard.

The crowd in a low murmur — not in my backyard.

The high priest raises his fist.

Not *IN MY* backyard.

Tiki torches are thrust upwards.

Not *IN MY* backyard.

Head thrown back and arms wide in a full-throated shout.

NOT IN MY BACKYARD!

NOT IN MY BACKYARD!

The crowd erupts into whoops and hollers.

Give 'em hell Bob!

The high priest lowers his hands and the camera drifts over to the Brylcreemed Lawrence Welk look-alike, standing stock-still with a malevolent grin.

We have such a lively and beautiful audience tonight. But I have to ask, do you have tired blood? Well, you need Geritol. It has twice the iron in a pound of calves liver. Geritol, the high potency tonic that strengthens the blood. Feel stronger in 7 days or your money back. Geritol. We are going to strike up the band now and play a little good time, easy beat for you all, a little something to forget, and take the pain away. Hit it, boys.

The band begins to swing with ancient mysteries vibrating along champagne strings — easy listening bubbles float effortless through the air, capturing the dancing mob in their shimmering curvature before DISSOLVING into the gray murk of concrete. INT. Camera bunker. The floor is littered with crumpled pages from *Sears* catalogs and the *Bulletin of the Atomic Scientists* — the corners are piled high with rusting soup cans and empties of Schlitz — the two rectangular camera portals face west towards distant Bikini, beyond where the sky meets the sea — cigarette burns and changeover cues. CUT TO the open door of the bunker — the camera peers out into overexposed daylight and begins to TRACK OUT — EXT. Airstrip — a dirt ribbon beaten out of the tropical vegetation — departures only. The improvised airfield is filled with small single-engine planes owned by rich explorers and corporate executives. A traffic jam of large trucks laden with cargo ties up the ramp as a mad scramble to load the planes plays out. Native men unload the trucks and pack the small planes full of palm trees, coconuts, shells, gold, sacred artifacts, parrots, women, children, and anything that isn't nailed down. White men in pith helmets and Hawaiian shirts smoke cigars and shoot the shit as they wait for their flights. An engine coughs and sputters to life OFFSCREEN — CLOSEUP on the sweating, overworked face of A MARSHALLESE PORTER — a main character from an unwritten script, the plot of which is unknown — he falls to the ground, dropping a crate of pearls that spill out across the runway. Two porters stop to check on him lying in the dirt, only to look up to see a man in a Hawaiin shirt tap his watch and make a gesture with his thumb towards the treeline. The two porters drape the fallen man over their shoulders and drag him over to the shade of the palms. They lay him down in the shadows next to the other dying islanders whose bodies inhabit the dark grove. A disease has broken out amongst the native population, they have developed symptoms similar to acute radiation poisoning — itching burning skin, wet lesions and bullae, hyperpigmented plaque, hair loss, nausea, vomiting, and diarrhea — some go into seizures while others fade in and out of consciousness, wracked with pain from wounds that won't heal — engines throttle up for takeoff — CUT TO CLOSEUP of sunken eyes that briefly flicker with life and the reflection of a great blue expanse of sky broken by a clogged freeway running like an artery into the heart of the suburbs — DISSOLVE to islands accessible by offramps with names like Levittown, Anaheim, Clear Lake City, Lemuria and Survival Town — prefabricated oases lined by landing strips and populated by colonists, patiently waiting for the day when the waves will swallow them whole. CUT TO SUNSET — the sound of an oxygen mask fills the sky. The pilot stands alone on the empty airstrip. Her flight suit is dusted in a thin snow of ash that slowly falls from the fire-streaked sky. There's no going back. CUT TO the bodies piled high beneath the palms. They begin to radiate a soft green glow that pulsates with the sound of the pilot's breath. Like phantoms, they rise and march towards the boneyard. They pick through the rusted fossils of Superfortresses and dreadnoughts, hauling their ancient bones back to the airstrip with supernatural ease. A shape takes form on the dirt runway in a MONTAGE of quiet industry — the ripped fuselage of two different planes, joined and patched by coconut timber and the bulkheads of destroyers — waterlogged turbosupercharged radial engines become brico-lages of steam engines, truck parts, and bamboo — silver wings now tarnished, trail hanging wire like a diseased carrion bird, the broken feathers of its airfoil covered in corrugated sheet metal — as the work comes to an end, the bomb bay doors open in SLOW MOTION and a line of irradiated ghosts take their place inside — SLOW TRACKING SHOT towards the torn cockpit, unreconstructed and dark in the failing light. Pilot needed on the set. And then I become the pilot — engines wheeze and whirl into life — the runway falling away below me — cruising altitude 31,000ft — easterly direction — the bombing run set. The film runs before me on a predetermined course over which I have no control. It runs on into the night, away from the sun and into the black.

And what else do you see?

Fire...Burning...

EXECUTIVE

kid, you'll never make it in Hollywood

FADE IN: (TITLE MUSIC)

141   END TITLE
                        FADE OUT.

Watch the Skies

CUT TO a test pattern whine that becomes the sturm and drang of library music soundtracking Americans staring into the sky as newspaper headlines make strafing runs down the center of their brains. SAUCERS OVER MIDWEST! UFOS COME TO DESTROY OUR WAY OF LIFE! The phone lines at the FBI tie themselves into knots, spurring the director into action.

V.O. Get me our best undercover agent.

That's me. I may not look like much but that's what I am — the best. The greatest undercover agent the Bureau has ever known. Hidden in plain sight. Waiting for the call. They don't call often but when they do, I answer. I was already on a case when *they* came for me — clean-cut boys in sharp suits who shook me out of a comfortable drunk I was curating in a St. Louis flophouse. I had been maintaining a cover as a former well-to-do reporter, an Ivy Leaguer who threw away daddy's money and a cushy front page career for literary ambitions that skidded and burst into flames on the runway. Having failed to sell my latest manuscript about the sick-sad-souls of the moneyed class, I had taken to passing out in gutters and writing ad copy for a local super-market circular, all the while secretly keeping my eye on local businessmen I suspected of being subversives. I was in the midst of preparing to stakeout a dumpster behind a market owned by a socialist rumored to be giving out free meals when the boys came for me.

V.O. Your job is to find these unidentified flying objects and make some sense of them. What are they? What do they mean? What do they want for Christ's sake? Are they the product of some unknown force or a Communist threat? Get out there and put your ears to the ground and see what you can dig up.

Consider me on the job. I was parachuted into Los Angeles in the dead of night where I started my investigation in a bottle of gin down on Skid Row. It was my only lead and it got me nowhere. I began to move across the country, bar to bar, floating on streams of smeared neon speech. A dive in every city contained a piece of the puzzle — a bartender in North Beach once saw a light in the sky, like a burning pyre, far to the west — a stripper wrapped her legs around me in Reno and told me there was a light at the end of the tunnel and that it felt cosmic and without end — a man with suspicious intent in Kenosha, lit my cigarette and revealed from out of his pocket a metal fragment of unknown origin — an unhappy young bride in Fort Worth cried into my cocktail about how she had heard a sad alien siren calling to her outside the window on her wedding night — I shared a bottle with three insurance salesmen in Little Rock who all swore up and down and on their children's graves, that they knew of a place outside of town where a mysterious science, so far advanced that it was almost magic, was practiced. I spent lifetimes collecting all these pieces and still nothing came together. The picture wasn't clear. That's the job though. No sense in crying. I reported in with graffiti on bathroom stalls. Coded messages and random phone numbers — CAME TO SHIT AND ONLY FARTED DISSOLVES INTO PHENOMENON WIDESPREAD BUT ELUSIVE, PLEASE ADVISE — FOR A GOOD TIME CALL YUR MOM KLD-340 — a receiver picks up and then the click of a tape spooling playback.

V.O. More sightings since last report. Saucers seen over national mall. Need more information. See what the other side is cooking with. Advertise yourself as an enemy agent. Infiltrate and keep your ears open — a soft slow chorus of *The Battle Hymn of The Republic* creeps in under the voice — on a personal note, the Bureau just wants you to know that you are doing a great service to your country. I am proud of you. Looking forward to your next evaluation. With your help, we will understand these things yet — CLICK.

Filled with a sense of purpose, I found my disguise out back in the trash can: three moth-eaten oversized coats, a pair of cracked salt-stained wellingtons, a dog-eared family bible, and an official Lone Ranger Fan Club hat and mask — this was deep cover. Incognito, I hit the streets of a planned suburb in New Jersey with a handwritten sign pasted with bible verses and began to scream that the end was nigh upon us. Sirens wailed and some hard-nosed cops picked me up on a not-in-my-backyard charge. They gave me a once over with their clubs and dropped me bleeding into a Hooverville inside of a blast crater at the center of Newark — an airburst of a low yield atomic weapon above 2,000FT left concrete buildings singed but intact. The post-blast conflagration had swept through the city center leaving burnt-out cars and hollowed-out structures where the walking dead drifted through the ruins. I was now among them. I passed out in the doorway of an abandoned building and woke up to the company of a destitute couple who shared a bottle of wine and no info — low-level agents. I drifted from fire to fire and continued to get nowhere. My guise allowed me to flow from east to west and north to south, my irregular orbits navigated by worn star maps. I hopped freight trains and stuck my thumb out on highways. I spent innumerable nights wrapped in newspapers, sleeping it off in bus stations waiting for Greyhounds. Those were the good nights. The mundane scenes that connected the bad ones. I remember I once got beat bloody and fell asleep in the snow outside Boulder, froze to death and woke up on a killing floor with a gym sock in my mouth and my brains splattered on the concrete in Chicago. Outside Cheyenne, I took two pumps full of birdshot to the back from a hobo hating railroad agent who watched as I DISSOLVED into a watery grave in a drainage ditch near

Bakersfield. I made the mistake once of stepping in front of a gang of kids speeding their souped-up Ford through The Nickel for kicks and broke every bone in my body. After crawling five miles on my belly through the LA river basin, I found a safe house in a storm drain where I cleaned up and took stock of the situation. Sometimes you have to dig deeper, I told myself. Start at the very bottom and work your way up, that's how great investigations are made and for this to be a great investigation, I'd have to work my way down to a depth far below the sewer. Put in some serious work. If only I had picked another profession I said to myself. I could have been anything — it's just unfortunate that I'm so damn good at this. The world is funny like that I guess. I stopped feeling sorry for myself and continued on my way. I died multiple times of pneumonia in a veterans hospital in downtown Los Angeles, sometimes alone and sometimes accompanied by a kind nurse who held my hand till the end. In one version, she whispered that the lights from above would soon be here to take me up and away. Her words filled me with warmth and I closed my eyes and I emerged like I always did, out of a shallow grave in a potter's field in Boyle Heights. I became a presence, dark and lumbering through brand new avenues with brand new cars parked in front of brand new homes. Children ran from me. Actresses shrieked in terror as I stalked day for night shots — under-exposed American nights — too dark to see. I must have done horrible things. But as the director says, what wouldn't I do to protect our way of life. I ended up not learning much. What I can say I know for sure is that the enemy is as in the dark as we are — nobody knows anything. My eventual report is going to be quite empty. A lot of leads but no answers. I thought I was on to something *once*. It was when a mysterious force played a piano for no one in Wichita. There I was vomiting on my shoes under the bar at last call when the lights came on and I realized that I was alone. Not a soul in sight. What had been a warm dank cave filled with cheap air, looked alien under the house lights. An unfamiliar planet. And there was this tune, emanating from the piano in the corner, coming in on a SLOW ZOOM and filled with static. Somewhere in the back of my mind, I knew the song but not the words. Had I forgotten them or had I never known them? Was it a memory or a message from the future? Where was I? A million light-years from home — freight trains in the night — the sonorous buzz of the Texaco sign — the concrete rhythm of an invisible freeway. I woke, sprawled out on a rocky beach somewhere north of Los Angeles. The cold Pacific under a gray sky. I watched as the waves came to drown the stones in the tide pools. Great frigid green rushes of saltwater that surged over and between algae stained rocks that had only mere seconds with which to breathe, to try to take in the warmth of the hidden sun, before being pounded again by another uncaring and ceaseless wave. I watched it all come in and watched it all go out. It doesn't stop. It only repeats. The same scene, over and over. In one take, I sat on the shore at low tide and watched pools of seagrass

swirl like hair in unseen currents. In another,
I stood on that beach as the wreckage of an
unknown craft washed ashore and cried while
smoke ran across the ground of Bronson Canyon.

CLOSEUP of a scaly claw rising from behind
the rocks—

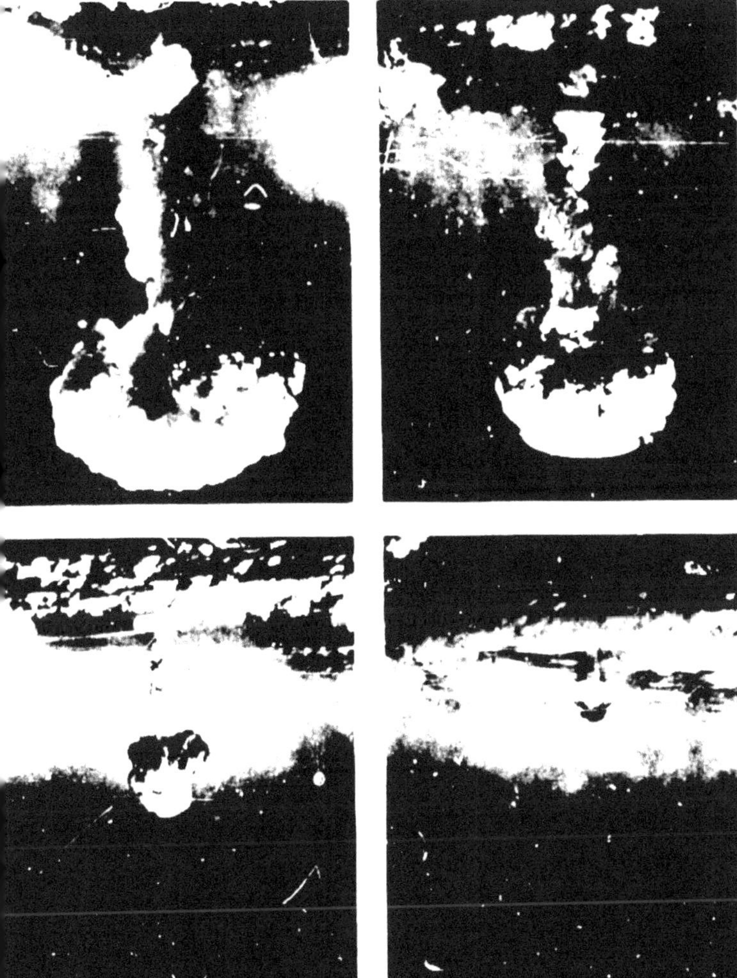

END

FILM

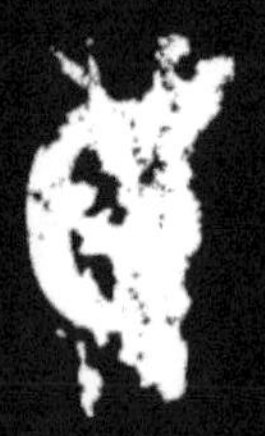